IN LUCIA'S EYES

Arthur Japin's first novel, *The Two Hearts of Kwasi Boachi*, was an international bestseller and has since been adapted for the stage, opera and a forthcoming film. *In Lucia's Eyes* went straight into the Dutch bestseller lists and won the prestigious Libris prize. Arthur Japin lives in Utrecht.

ARTHUR JAPIN

In Lucia's Eyes

TRANSLATED FROM THE DUTCH BY
David Colmer

VINTAGE BOOKS
London

Published by Vintage 2006

2 4 6 8 10 9 7 5 3

Copyright © Arthur Japin 2003
Translation © David Colmer 2005

Arthur Japin has asserted his right under the Copyright,
Designs and Patents Act, 1988 to be identified as the author
of this work

First published in Dutch by De Arbeiderspers as
Een schitterend gebrek 2003

Publication has been made possible with the financial
support of the Foundation for the Production and
Translation of Dutch Literature

First published in Great Britain in 2005 by
Chatto & Windus

Vintage
Random House, 20 Vauxhall Bridge Road,
London SW1V 2SA

Random House Australia (Pty) Limited
20 Alfred Street, Milsons Point, Sydney,
New South Wales 2061, Australia

Random House New Zealand Limited
18 Poland Road, Glenfield, Auckland 10, New Zealand

Random House (Pty) Limited
Isle of Houghton, Corner of Boundary Road & Carse O'Gowrie,
Houghton, 2198, South Africa

Random House Publishers India Private Limited
301 World Trade Tower, Hotel Intercontinental Grand Complex,
Barakhamba Lane, New Delhi 110 001, India

The Random House Group Limited Reg. No. 954009
www.randomhouse.co.uk/vintage

A CIP catalogue record for this book
is available from the British Library

ISBN 9780099479031 (from Jan 2007)
ISBN 0099479036

Papers used by Random House are natural,
recyclable products made from wood grown in
sustainable forests. The manufacturing processes
conform to the environmental regulations of the
country of origin

Printed and bound in Great Britain by
Cox & Wyman Limited, Reading, Berkshire

For Elsa

'Many things that exist only in the imagination
later become real.' G.C.

Contents

I

The Benefit of Love

If there's one thing I'm good at, it's loving. That might not seem much, but I'm proud of it. I learnt it the way a stray dog learns to swim: by being stuffed in a gunnysack with the rest of the litter and thrown into a fast-flowing river.

The one that survived against the odds, that's me. With the yelps of the drowned still ringing in my ears, I had to learn to love.

I didn't go under.

I made it to the side.

I love.

Other people carry their sorrow in their heart. Unseen, it hollows them out from within. My salvation was that I wear my sorrow on the outside, where no one can miss it.

I

Amsterdam 1758

The evening on which I came to see everything in a new light, I was actually intending to dine, as I did every Thursday, with Mr Jamieson, a wholesaler of skins and tobacco, and possibly go out dancing together afterwards. It was only after an attack of gout had forced the good man to cancel our appointment that I decided to visit my box at the theatre.

Don't misunderstand me, I am not used to luxury. Since the calamity struck, I have been at life's mercy and very frugal. I had to be. For a long time I had no idea what the next day would bring. Whether I would have to go hungry. Whether anyone would shelter me. Whether I would be attacked and forced to move on. Even after finally attaining a certain status in Amsterdam, I always confined myself to the clothing expected in the circles in which I moved and the extras I needed to practise my profession. I never allowed myself any extravagance. It wasn't even something I missed. In the last couple of years, however, I have permitted myself this one thing: a permanent seat in a box at the French theatre on the Overtoom.

I was on my way there that evening in mid-October. As usual, I had hired a small but respectable boat. There was a chill in the air. In Amsterdam the cold on the canals is worse than it is in Venice. It sets in months earlier, it's more piercing and insidious, and it tends to settle in the bones rather than the lungs. I still prefer a boat to a carriage. The people on the quays ignore those who pass them on the water. More or less unnoticed, I am able to study others at my leisure. On the evening in question I was doing just that, partly for my own pleasure and partly for professional reasons.

In the curve of the Herengracht, two gentlemen caught my eye. One of them, I already knew: Jan Rijgerbos, a dealer in stocks. A friendly, cultivated widower, Rijgerbos is fit, well built and undemanding. His companion was unknown to me. He had a dark face and a striking profile. It was the latter which immediately attracted me. His appearance touched me in a way I could not explain. I asked the boatman to row faster so that we could keep up with the two men, and studied the stranger. He had an oval face and a blond wig that showed it to advantage. Although not particularly handsome, he aroused my desire.

This annoyed me.

I am the one who arouses desire.

He was too skinny for me anyway, I decided. What's more, he was dressed according to the latest Paris fashion – in breeches of yellow silk that showed his calves – and cut an absurd figure in such bleak weather. I lost interest and began looking around for other pedestrians. As we passed under the Leidsebrug, Rijgerbos and his friend were just crossing it and I managed to catch a snatch of their conversation. They were speaking French: one with difficulty, the other fluently. I liked the sound of the Frenchman's voice and ordered the boatman to stop beneath the arches of the bridge. There we waited in the shadows until the two men were out of sight.

If it were not for the recklessly low neckline I was wearing; if it were not that I am anything but free of sin; if it were not that my thoughts that evening were far from elevated; if it were not for my being the kind of woman a higher power would not squander ten minutes of His precious time on; if it were not for any of these things, you might think that God, or maybe the devil, had arranged the whole thing for His entertainment. A coincidence like this! How rarely are we allowed a glimpse of the grand context within which the events of our lives take place. Even years of being buffeted by Fate had not prepared me for what lay ahead. All that time I had been constantly on my guard. And now, just when I thought that life had finally grown bored and stopped bandying me about, it rose up again in all its intensity and seized me by the throat.

This time I have no choice but to accept that some catastrophes do have a meaning. It *does* make sense to persevere. I have been provided with the proof of that. Or, at least, God willing . . . that proof will soon be provided.

As usual I took my seat shortly after the start of the performance, to offend as few people as possible. The opera was an old pastoral play that had recently been put to music by a composer from Grenoble. The cast was filled with the theatre's regular singers, and ovations welcomed the favourites. The lead, a shepherdess, was being played by a soprano who had triumphed in this role all over Europe.

Midway through the first act, Jan Rijgerbos knocked on the door of my box.

'What a surprise,' I said, 'I had no idea you liked the theatre. I don't recall ever seeing you here before.'

He was too well bred to show his discomfort at talking to me, but he did take care to remain out of sight from the auditorium. I am used to that. It didn't hurt my feelings and I didn't hold it against him.

'I must confess that the music is too mannered to my ear, but what do I know of it? No, I have a guest, a friend from France.

He is visiting our city as an agent of the French treasury and insists on attending the theatre every evening, as he does in Paris. We were in the pit . . .'

Rijgerbos stepped aside to reveal his guest, whom he introduced as Monsieur le Chevalier de Seingalt.

'They sold us those seats in the pit with the assurance that they provided the best view of the performance,' the man said in French, bowing to kiss my hand. 'But no one warned us that the evening's most beguiling presence would not be on stage.'

There is nothing a man can say to a woman that I haven't heard before. Compliments about appearances always depress me, especially on a first meeting. As soon as they are uttered, their obligatory nature seems to weary them. They have been dispatched on a mission they have no faith in, as heavy as plough-horses trying to perform dressage. Some women live for sweet talk. I would rather go without. But how is a man supposed to understand something like that? He hopes to please us.

I cordially invited the gentlemen to join me in the box. Jan concealed himself behind the curtain, but Seingalt stepped forward without embarrassment and stood there in full view of the rest of the audience. The yellow silk of his conspicuous suit seemed to light up in the glow of the footlights.

It was only when he was sure that all eyes were upon us, that he sat down and deliberately slid his chair closer to mine. This could only mean one of two things: either Jan had told him nothing about me, or he had told him everything and Monsieur le Chevalier was an absolute fire-eater. Either way, I decided to like him.

We listened to the rest of the aria in silence. All the while I was aware of Seingalt looking at me. He was trying to make out the outline of my face through the lace I was wearing as a veil. Although I knew he would not succeed, his attempt disturbed me. I had to control my breathing to avoid betraying my excitement. His eyes, large and black under heavy lids, kept

8

wandering, sometimes down over my body, sometimes up in the hope of catching my expression.

When the big chandeliers were lit for the interval, I moved aside to stay in the shadows. The chevalier informed me that he was staying in L'Etoile d'Orient, on the corner of the Nes and the Kuipersteeg. He told me that he had recently arrived from Paris with the task of easing France's financial position by selling French government bonds in Amsterdam as their price had fallen too much at home because of the war. All the while he kept trying to make out the expression on my face. To no avail. Eventually he asked what no one else in his position had dared to ask: whether I would reward him for the friendship he offered by allowing him a glimpse of my countenance. He was clearly unused to a woman refusing him anything, because later he tried again, less politely. Finally he asked straight out why I begrudged him something he desired so deeply.

'If you owned a valuable gem,' I said, 'you wouldn't put it on display for every Tom, Dick and Harry to look at, would you?'

'No, you're right, I would keep it somewhere safe.'

'That is just how I watch over myself, monsieur. Carefully.'

One day I decided to start wearing a veil. Its effect on men is remarkable. More than anything else, men want that which has been forbidden them. A man will crave whatever you deny him. Given a choice, he will always take the unknown.

'This gem you hide must be unique in the world,' the saviour of France pouted, letting his gaze glide mischievously down my bare throat, 'considering the fact that you have no qualms about exposing other treasures that Tom, Dick and Harry would kill for.'

'Give up, sir,' I mocked, 'you have met your match.'

I toyed with him a little longer until he fell silent and pretended that the singers, who had returned to the stage, were demanding his attention. To keep his hopes up, I opened my fan and laid it on the plush before him, a sign that is understood all over Europe.

For years I was accustomed to seeing myself in the eyes of others. I let myself be defined by the way they reacted to me. The looks they gave me told me who I was. Then I hit upon the idea of shielding myself from all that.

At first I covered my face only to go out. By constraining myself in this fashion, I experienced a freedom I could only remember from my earliest childhood. Since then, I live as reborn. As long as I am not seen by others, I have no need to look at myself. Delivered from the image I have of myself, I can once again move through the world without danger, like a child among grown-ups. They no longer see me as one of them and let me get away with more as a result. I don't have to join in their seriousness. While they sit at the table, I imagine myself crawling around on the floor between their legs. Children are aware of the judgement of adults, but it doesn't weigh them down. In my disguise, I rediscovered that light-heartedness. It pleased me so much that in the last few years I have kept my veil on almost constantly, even at home, sometimes even when alone. I always wrap myself in it while working. It's what has made me so successful.

The play takes a dramatic turn. The squire warns the shepherdess: his son may be in love with her, but he will disinherit him if they marry. To preserve her sweetheart's happiness, she pretends to love another. Then abandons her flock and joins a convent. Just after she has become a bride of Christ, the lovesick youth comes knocking at the gate. He has seen through the whole scheme, but too late. One last time he sees her beauty. Then she dons her wimple and is lost to him for ever.

'What mutilation!' sighed Seingalt, as the soprano disappeared under her habit. His indignation was genuine and the words just slipped out. 'Hiding something so beautiful, that must surely count as a mortal sin!'

'I am happy to leave the judgement of our sins, monsieur, to He who invented them.'

He looked at me and burst out laughing.

'Perhaps He can take the same opportunity to explain to me why someone like you would choose to hide herself.'

Soon after, I closed my fan and put it away. Heroines who sacrifice themselves unnecessarily should not count on my sympathy. Geese who let their minds overrule their emotions annoy me, and I am always glad to see them get their just deserts. Rather than sit out the rest of the act, I asked the gentlemen to excuse me. The pastoral was upsetting me, and I go to the opera to be entertained, not shaken.

I have often been accused of hiding myself behind my veil, but the opposite is true.

I hide the world.

I have lowered a curtain in front of it.

Through that haze of lace and silk it looks so much gentler.

2

I don't remember any boundaries. Pasiano, the estate where I was born, extended out over the hills as far as the eye could see. The doors were always open. I could walk for hours and, whichever way I went, everything was familiar. My parents never worried about me. In the morning, when I raced off after a bird or a butterfly, they weren't scared to see me disappear out of sight. They knew that by midday the smells spreading out over the fields from the kitchens would lure me home for lunch. While still young I befriended the horses in the meadows, and in time they let me ride them, with my hands in their manes and my heels in their flanks. The chicks from the fowl yard were my toys and the overseer's dogs were my playmates. Together we rolled down the golden slopes and ran through the woods. The streams in the valleys were warm and shallow, and until my tenth birthday the gamekeepers were forbidden from setting traps. At Pasiano there was no danger. There were no limits to my happiness. I spent my childhood unafraid and unjudged.

I had no reason to believe that things in the rest of the world were any different.

Like everyone else, I felt before I thought. It was only after people had begun to teach me, that I learnt to distinguish and name facts. But I never placed what I was taught above the things I knew intuitively. Even now, I am reluctant to admit to reality. I like to delude myself that everything is still possible. I have a talent for that. If the devil were staring straight at me, I could still convince myself that my visitor was an angel. I'm such a dab hand at it, I could even set Lucifer to doubting. It makes me feel less scared.

I believe in dreams. For the first fourteen years of my life, I lived one. I understand them. They feel familiar. That doesn't mean I don't see the truth. I actually see it much too clearly. I screw up my eyes to shut out the glare. That lets me feel secure a little longer, even with the smell of sulphur already burning in my nose.

Those first few years I thought that Pasiano was ours. From the grain fields of Squazaré, where the sun rises, to Rivarotta, where the storks settle down for the winter in November. From the deer wood near Codopé up to Azzanello, where the sun disappears at night behind the ruined castle of the Montefeltri. I simply had no reason to think that my own world did not belong to me.

In reality, the estate was owned by the Countess of Montereale, who spent the summer months there for her health. She had a husband, Count Antonio, whom she loved passionately even though he lived in Milan with his mistress. The countess had a daughter, Adriana, but we seldom saw her because she stayed in Venice with her tutor, a Frenchman called Monsieur de Pompignac.

Compared to the wealth of most noble families, the Montereales' fortune was modest. Without unremitting attention and years of careful planning, Adriana would not have stood the slightest chance in the matrimonial market.

The competition in the upper echelons of Venetian society is killing. To attain a position in those circles, a girl has to shine at all of the big parties, not just during the season but in the summer as well: at the country homes on the Brenta and at the most important summer residences elsewhere in the Veneto.

Without her daughter to keep her company, the countess felt lonely at Pasiano and had a lot of love to spare. She directed it at me. She was used to having me around and she liked it when I played in the drawing room. Even when she had guests, if she looked out through the French windows and saw me on the lawn, she would call me in and take me on her lap. I called her aunt and assumed she was part of our family.

One day in spring, one of her cousins came to stay. He was fleeing an outbreak of smallpox in Chioggia and had brought his young son with him. Like me, the boy was six years old. We became friends. I showed him my paradise, but he didn't seem to see it. I picked out a downy chick from the fowl yard and gave it to him as a gift, but he shrugged and let it go again. Near the rapids, I showed him how you could catch the dragonflies that danced in the spray without hurting them. Fascinated, he accepted the insect I offered him and declared that he intended to become a surgeon. He then broke the creature's wings so that he could practise tying on splints. Later, he climbed onto one of the dogs and tried to spur the animal by kicking it with his heels. It bit him. To me that only seemed fair. The dog didn't draw blood, but the boy still made a big show of it. He ran to his father and demanded that the overseer put down all his animals that same day. The father personally watched while they were put into gunnysacks. I was inconsolable. The countess pulled me over to her on the couch, embraced me as if she might lose me too, and rocked me passionately.

'You see, my dear,' she whispered. 'You see what happens when you let someone get too close to the things you love.'

Soon after, the boy left for Gemona with his father, ostensibly because the dreaded disease they were fleeing did not affect higher regions. In reality, the countess had asked her cousin to leave. He blamed me for that and, climbing into the coach, exclaimed spitefully that it was irresponsible to allow highborn children to play with the daughter of a kitchenmaid.

That evening my mother explained the difference between servants and nobles. She told me that the countess was not really my aunt and that we had no power over what happened on the estate. Instead, we lived there as subordinates, dependent on the kindness of the owner.

This made no difference to my life at Pasiano. I was as free as ever in the fields and woods, and I still had the run of the manor. It was no less precious to me. The Countess of Montereale loved me just as much as ever. But still, a sorrow had been born. It wasn't something I had imagined. All of the next summer it shimmered in the wheat, and that winter I heard it in the honking of the geese.

Few people fathom the power of a word. Just one, spoken without thinking, can change the world. The truth is more than just the things you see. That is why its value is only relative. I am very careful with it.

My mother wasn't actually a maid. She and my father ran the household, and she was personally responsible for the domestic staff and the well-being of guests.

My father's family had been in the service of the Montereales for five generations when my mother visited the estate as a young girl in 1728. There was never any intention of her staying. At the time she was apprenticed to her father and had travelled with him to supervise the installation of the gigantic mirrors he had designed for the grand salon at

Pasiano. The heavy work was carried out by a few of the local foresters who had been temporarily excused from their usual duties for this purpose – my father was one of them. Despite the cold they took off their shirts and worked up such a sweat installing the gigantic works of art that the salon windows steamed over.

My grandfather's fame extended far beyond Venezia Giulia. His designs can be found from Vienna to Milan. He made his mirrors by applying a technique he had learnt on journeys to Tiflis and Constantinople: instead of cutting the front of the glass, he did his engraving on the back, before applying the mercury. Even the great Tiepolo admired his work, and his sumptuous designs evoked an illusion of extraordinary depth. There seemed to be another, intangible, dimension behind the glass. Dazzling and fey, it caught and reflected the light in ways the people in our region had never seen before. Season after season, it was fashionable to have your house decorated by my grandfather. He embellished paintings, windows and doors with his engraved mirrors, and his wealthy patrons tried to astonish their guests by having tables and even chairs blown from glass so that my grandfather could transform them with his secret procedure. In those years boudoirs and salons everywhere were filled with baubles he had decorated in this fashion. His popularity reached its peak when he developed a method of applying copper powder and gold foil to the back of the glass, imbuing the mirror with a gentle glow, so that anyone who looked into it saw a flattering image of themselves without their everyday blemishes and imperfections. The great families of Venice valued his work even more highly than glass from Murano, so to this day all those who look into the mirrors of the Mocenigo, Venier and Zorzi palaces see a gentler version of themselves framed by intangible apparitions drawn by my grandfather. By the time I was born, the aristocracy had long since moved on to a new fad. My grandfather's fame was a thing of the past. That didn't bother him. Success had exhausted him. After years of working to order, he was happy to return to the fount of his skill, pleasing no one but himself. Instead of working as a craftsman, he was now an artist. The things he made were no longer in demand except with a few faithful customers, people of taste who shared his fascination and occasionally commissioned him, among them, the Countess of Montereale, who chose to mark the birth of her daughter by refurbishing the ballroom at Pasiano.

The work took five full weeks.

That was when it happened.

'You had me in agonies,' my mother would upbraid my father. 'That divine glass in those coarse peasant's hands! It's a miracle we're not living between shards. Entrusting something like that to you, I don't know what I was thinking!' Meanwhile the look in her eyes betrayed the fact that she still knew very well and was relishing the memory. 'What would a clod like you know about something fragile and refined?' She often acted out tirades like this to provoke my father into grabbing her by the waist with those big hands of his, just as he had done back then. She succeeded effortlessly. In no time he had seized hold of her and was lifting her up while she shrieked with laughter.

'Let go of me, you big oaf!' she screamed. 'Are you trying to break me? You want me to give myself to you? I'd sooner give a crystal chalice full of honey to a bear!' Knowing all the while that my father would respond by roughly licking her face. My parents were not at all embarrassed to do this in front of me; in fact they seemed to act out the whole performance just to show me how fiercely the love that I had sprung from still raged within them.

'I noticed that father of yours ogling me those first few days decorating the salon,' she explained later, when I was in love myself. It was the first and only time we spoke together not as mother and daughter, but as friends. I was fourteen.

Her confidences made me feel uncomfortable, but I was glad she took me seriously. No one understood love as well as she did, and she realised that, as young as I was, I had met mine.

'He never once looked straight at me,' she related, 'the sluggard, but I kept catching his eye in the mirrors he was carrying. At first I felt flattered, but after a few days, when he still hadn't made a move, I got fed up with it. He was so pigheaded it was infuriating. I grew jealous of my own reflection. I waited until my father had left for lunch with the other workmen and asked him what he meant by eyeing me so brazenly. He had to summon up all his courage to answer. "I wasn't looking at you," he mumbled, and even then he still had the nerve to speak to the glass instead of me. I got angry. "It's because of your father's artistry," he said, "it's so mysterious and incomprehensible I can see my future in it." I snorted contemptuously and was about to walk away. I've never thought much of that kind of drivel, but it turned out he meant it. He grabbed my wrist so hard it hurt. "I'm sorry," he said, "but I don't dare to avert my eyes from my good fortune for a single moment." He refused to let me go until I had seen what he was referring to. This was his clumsy way of forcing me to look at myself. A glimpse wasn't enough, no, he ordered me to stare into my own eyes. He sounded threatening. I grew scared. I was afraid that he might have come from one of those Alpine peasant families that are inbred to the point of lunacy. The safest thing was to obey him. I looked at myself. And kept looking. It wasn't easy. Don't forget, I grew up in a workshop full of mirrors. No matter where I looked, I could always see myself. I thought I had a good idea of what I looked like, but now I saw something else. Not better or worse, but more complete. Suddenly I realised that I had never taken in more than my outline and had always avoided looking myself in the eye. I can't explain it any other way. Until then I had seen my likeness as if I were an amateur completing a painting:

detailed but dead. But now I saw my portrait the way a great artist might capture it in a quick sketch, not by showing everything, but by giving the little he does show a radiance that betrays a beating heart and warm, rapid breathing. Eventually the madman relaxed his grip. I looked at him. His eyes were filled with tears. That was all there was to it. "It's all right," I told him. "I saw it." '

Then my mother rocked me for a while, knowing it would be the last time. Finally, she kissed me as a sign that our intimate conversation was over, and spoke in a voice that was suddenly resolute and factual, as if she wanted to round off my entire upbringing. 'That's the only thing that counts, darling, someone seeing more in you than you ever imagined there was to see.'

The young lovers in the salon could not conceal their happiness. As soon as my grandfather returned from his lunch break, he saw that he would have to let his daughter go. The radiant couple pleased the Countess of Montereale so much that she refused to let them leave for Pordenone after the mirror room was completed. Instead, she offered them a position as the housekeepers of Pasiano.

That was how I came to be born that same year in an enormous four-poster bed in one of the second-floor guest rooms. On the day of my birth, my grandfather made a small round mirror. It hung above my cradle like a glittering toy. Facets cut into the edge refracted the light and sent all the colours of the rainbow dancing over my bedlinen and the curtains of my cradle. That cherished object is the only one of my possessions that I have held onto through everything. The decoration is simple: a garland of vines held up by four small cherubs. In the deepest layer of the glass, visible only in direct light, a dish has been engraved, with on it the eyes that are the symbol of the saint I was named after, *Santa Lucia*.

3

The autumn storms reached Holland early that year. In all my time in Amsterdam, I hadn't seen anything like it. Seven boats sank on the Zuider Zee. Two broke up in dock. Five people were buried alive when a house collapsed on the Keizersgracht, and God knows how many died across the Jordan, where an entire block was consumed by a fire that the wind kept raging for three whole days. To top it all, the spring tide breached the seawall. The dike-grave's guard repaired it that same night, but the series of disasters weighed heavily on the city.

On Friday there was a lull, but the threat was not yet over. Around half past three, we heard a town crier. He stood on the corner and announced that all chimneys that were out of plumb were to be pulled down immediately, as more gales were expected.

Giovanna and Danae looked at me in the mirror. I was standing next to them. We were in the process of making ourselves beautiful. The girls had been working hard all week and had spent a lot of time indoors. The rooms I provide are small, and we all felt like going out. The two girls, who both come from Parma, didn't know another soul in Amsterdam and lived under my protection. They had set their hearts on visiting a music hall. The storm had confined all vessels to harbour and the city was overflowing with sailors and ship's captains; the two friends were keen to try their luck. I myself had been invited to dine with Jan Rijgerbos. His request had been friendly and highly promising. I didn't want to disappoint him. We decided to ignore the weather and persevere with our plans. In fact we had little choice. Times were hard. I used Spanish paper to apply a light blush over my protégées' white lead and chose the correct beauty spot for each. Then I laced their corsets and they laced mine. I put on a dress of deep-blue chintz. They chose a thinner fabric that accentuated their youthfulness, and we admired ourselves in the mirror. I felt strong and beautiful, and wanted to keep it that way. For this evening I chose a purple veil, embroidered in Bruges by the nuns of St Anne's.

Jan called for me at my home. To my surprise, he didn't take me to his residence on the Herengracht or to one of the establishments where he dared to be seen with me. Instead we followed the Amstel to the family's country house at Ouderkerk. There we found a small group of friends sitting in front of the fire. I recognised two gentlemen: Rindert Bolhuys, the sexton of the South Church, with whom I had occasionally risked a jig, and my friend Jamieson, the merchant from Massachusetts. They were listening to a stranger, who was in the middle of telling a story. He had his back turned to me, but I knew his voice. It was the Frenchman from the opera. He was halfway through an account of the *grisettes* of Paris, young women who eked out a living by the sweat of their brow.

Jan noticed me flinch, but held me firmly by the arm.

'What have you arranged?' I asked.

'Don't be so touchy. It's only a little entertainment.'

'I like clarity. Your letter did not mention any others. I was expecting an evening alone with you, as usual.'

'Blame Monsieur de Seingalt. He insisted on seeing you again.'

At that moment the Frenchman noticed me. He concluded his story by saying that common girls like these were better off than ladies of breeding because they were able to live independently, free of the restraints of polite society. Instead of reaping his success, he abandoned his audience to come over to greet me.

'Have no illusions,' Jan whispered. 'He's already courting an alderman's daughter. Still, for days now, he hasn't stopped asking about you.'

'What have you told him?'

'Everything,' he said reassuringly, 'except the truth.'

We dined together, then retired to the drawing room for some music. The gentlemen discussed financial matters and affairs of state. Mr Jamieson was asked about the progress of the British war against the French and Indians in Canada. He called the conflict a blessing for New York, a city where he had recently acquired several warehouses and planned to settle in the near future.

'Money is streaming in from all sides,' he said, 'to pay and maintain the troops. For a merchant like me, who makes his fortune where it is to be made, these are golden times. In just a few years the harbour has outgrown Boston's, and the streets are grander than Philadelphia's. There are twelve churches there now and several hundred stores at least.'

'Is it not true,' asked Bolhuys bluntly, 'that a lot of strange characters gravitate there, riff-raff that wouldn't be tolerated anywhere else?'

'People from all over the world do go to the city to try their luck, that's true. The restless atmosphere is ideal for those who wish to escape their past . . .'

'And which married man wouldn't?' exclaimed Jan cheerfully.

'. . . and anyone who wants to reinvent himself.'

'I have been told,' announced Seingalt, who naturally took the side of the French, 'that there are more slaves in your city than in the other Northern states and that their uprising was quashed even more brutally than it was in the South. What, do you think, will be left of your prosperity if France triumphs and grants the Negroes their liberty?'

'That, monsieur, would be as catastrophic as a rain of glowing coals,' Jamieson replied, 'and just as likely.'

After this, the men spent some time discussing the constant discord between the two nations. I tried to remain aloof and entertain myself with the other guests, but no one failed to notice that the two men were in complete disagreement about everything, whether it be Catholic Confession, the consumption of raw fish or the various uses of citrus fruit. The debate grew dangerously heated when Seingalt announced that he considered the influence of the Duke of Brunswick over the Dutch Crown Prince Willem a menace because of the partisan way he preferred England to France. His words were so piqued and curt that I began to believe him jealous at having to share my favours with Jamieson. After his outburst, the company thought it better to confine the conversation to pleasantries, and the other gentlemen began alluding to Seingalt's virility and conquests. He distracted attention away from this subject with an account of the national lottery for the École Militaire, which he had set up together with d'Alembert and Diderot, and a long story about the attempted assassination of Louis XV, an event he claimed to have experienced at first hand by virtue of his employment as a secret agent of the court. In short, the chevalier revealed himself as a man who was able to get completely carried away by his own stories.

When he had warmed everyone up, he set up a game with

magic squares and pyramids. Radiating complete conviction, he presented it as a key to the interpretation of the cabbala. Jan confided in me that Seingalt had performed the same trick with great success at the courts of Europe, where many people had unreservedly believed the things he had told them. One could ask a question, the letters of which he would assign a numerical value. He then conjured with these numbers until answers appeared. The answers, too, were in a numerical alphabet of his own devising, but at the same time he claimed to have no influence over the result at all. I must say that he played his role masterfully, making it easy to believe that he really was receiving messages and answers from an oracle or power beyond himself. Several of those present were genuinely anxious to hear what the future had in store for them. Seingalt wanted to do one of these predictions for me too, but I declined the offer, telling him that I preferred to learn my lessons from the past.

Around ten o'clock it became necessary to close the shutters. The trees were still in full leaf and the recent storm had already uprooted several along the river. Now that the wind was rising again, there was a danger that the rest might fall as well. We were asked, for our own safety, to leave the drawing room, which was adjacent to the dike. Most of the company chose to return to the city, among them Mr Jamieson, who offered to take me home, but I told him that I would rather stay a little longer to listen to the Frenchman.

'To each his own,' grumbled Jamieson, 'but how can you trust a nation that never stops scoffing onions? It disturbs the sleep. No wonder there's not a man left in Paris who hasn't traded his dreams for a belief.'

Those who chose to remain spread out through the other rooms. The Chevalier de Seingalt ensconced himself with me in one of the antechambers. No one disturbed us there and as soon as the civilities were out of the way he made his move.

I must admit, his technique betrayed an impressive

knowledge of the female soul. Now that we were alone, he didn't say another word about his own adventures. Self-effacing, he asked about me, my habits and desires, my thoughts, my faith, my beliefs, my past . . . I didn't enlighten him about any of these things, but he persevered: Where had I spent my childhood? How had I learnt such excellent French? Did I have family in Holland? Wasn't it lonely without relations nearby? Did I find solace in religion or rely on myself? There was no stopping him. Above all else, he gave the impression of being fascinated by every facet of my mind. This is a technique for the advanced practitioner, but I saw through it effortlessly. Of all the arts of seduction, it is the gentlest and, therefore, generally the most effective.

Not today.

In anyone else this attempt would have aroused my sympathy, but coming from Seingalt it annoyed me. I could not bear the fact that his interest in me was feigned. I realised that I had wanted it to be genuine and this, in turn, made me disappointed with myself. Is it any wonder that a man cannot possibly understand a woman? In short: we didn't get on. I had no intention of revealing any aspect of myself to him at all. Since he persisted and played his part convincingly, I decided to go over to the offensive.

'Are you always so roundabout as to undress a woman intellectually before starting on her body?'

'Her body?' he asked as if I had said it in Turkish. 'A woman can give her body to anyone. I have no interest in that.'

'And you pretend to be a man?'

'My challenge is to win a woman's heart.'

'How praiseworthy,' I mocked. 'And? Do you win many?'

'Until now? Almost without exception.'

He seemed to enjoy my brazenness.

'Wonderful,' I continued. 'One of these women gives you her heart. You accept it. Bravo and I hope you enjoy it. But then? What do you do with the prize? Where do you keep it, once you have it in your possession? You love a while, and then? Where do you leave it when you go off on your next hunting expedition? Do you nail it to the wall of your trophy room with the rest of the game you've shot or do you toss it over your shoulder to see where it lands?'

'I have never wronged any of the women I have known. I have never left a single woman behind unhappy.'

'Not one?'

'Not one!'

'I wish I were young and naive enough to believe you.'

'Why should I lie?'

'Goodness, why would a man lie about love?' I asked, feigning an exasperating foolishness. 'Let me think . . .'

'What made you so cynical?'

'I have seen enough men at work to know what they do with discarded female hearts.'

'My lovers and I have parted as friends, without exception.'

'Of course, you very kindly swept the pieces together and gave the shattered heart back to the poor thing.'

'Never, I tell you!'

He held up his hands like a little boy who has been at the porridge pot but has an expression of such innocence on his face that you can't help but forgive him, even though he's still licking the last remnants from the corner of his mouth.

'When lovers go their own way,' he explained, 'it must be by mutual agreement. No anger. No jealousy.'

'And if the woman in question doesn't want to? What if she loves you and wants to keep you?'

'Then it becomes a matter of finding a better man for her. She will fall for his charms and make the decision herself.'

'No broken hearts.'

'I'm very precise about that. I see it as a matter of life and death. If someone I loved were sorrowful after my departure, the whole affair would have failed. Rather than considering it a victory, I would see it as a defeat.'

'Well thank God you have been spared such an experience,' I said, 'unless . . .' – and to increase the effect I hesitated as long as possible – '. . . couldn't it be possible that the women you left simply chose not to tell you about their sorrow?'

'Why should they lie?'

'They loved you, didn't they?'

'Exactly,' he said contentedly, as if that proved his point. 'Surely one needn't have any qualms about telling the truth to the person one loves?'

'That piece of logic, sir, contradicts the enormous experience you boast of. Honesty is not love's strongest suit.'

He made his face drop.

'Ah,' he said shaking his head, 'now you've exposed yourself after all.'

'Perhaps a woman would prefer to remain silent, taking the honourable way out with a fond farewell. By leaving the man's delusion of victory intact, the woman masks her own defeat.'

He considered this, and the thought clearly annoyed him.

'You seem to know a lot about defeat,' he said, needled. 'Are you such an expert in that area?'

'Unfortunately.'

'I'm sorry, but it's hardly surprising! You take cheerfulness so seriously. What on earth do you have against it? It refreshes the spleen and cleanses the blood. How can you hope for happiness when you make love a hanging offence?'

'That's a fine rebuke!' I said. 'Just a moment ago you were the one who was attributing such crucial importance to love.'

'Fortunately, there are enough women who derive pleasure from it in the same way as a man.'

'Have you ever stopped to think that they might be

playing along to avoid seeming childish? That they submit to a man so as not to be bettered?'

His body stiffened, as if he had been hit. While he let the scope of the idea sink in, the disbelief in his eyes made way for determination as his protestations changed to anger. Finally he tapped into this new source of strength.

'But what kind of woman are you? Have you set your mind to cheating me of all pleasure for ever? I challenge you: if I have ever wronged one woman, I will make amends for it. I will give up everything and marry her.'

'You think that in order to marry, you must give up everything. And you call me a cynic?'

'I will give up the life I lead and be hers for the rest of my days.'

'You forget, you are a man.'

'Love is my only religion. The thought that I could hurt someone with it is terrible.'

'So you would do that? End the merry life you lead, if I proved that a woman, even just one, has fallen victim to her love for you.'

'I swear it.'

'Take care. I am tempted to keep you to your word.'

'One woman, just one from all the women I have loved, who reproaches me for something afterwards. Try to find one, but I can tell you now: she doesn't exist. You would have more luck turning sulphur into gold.'

'The alchemy of love is dangerous. I have seen it produce stranger transformations.'

'Or better still, put me to the test yourself, madame. Give me the benefit of your love. Allow me to win you and see whether it pleases you, you who have apparently suffered so grievously at the hands of us men.'

Words were burning on my lips, but I swallowed them.

'We can make a game of it,' he insisted, 'and place a wager

on the result, if you like. It may very likely alleviate your boredom for an evening or two.'

I assumed an air of indifference, opened a book that was lying on the table and leafed through it.

'A man who has never wronged a *single* woman,' I said after a while, 'how very unusual! How did you manage to achieve such a miracle?'

'By placing free will above all else. I only want a woman's heart when she offers it to me herself. That is not altogether selfless. In my experience, lust is most enjoyable when it is satisfied gladly and avidly. A woman who loves does not hesitate to give herself. She is open in every sense of the word.'

'And do you give yourself to her with that same abandon?'

'If only,' he said and was silent in turn. He poked the fire, although it was already roaring. Then he admitted, 'I was deprived of that ability long ago.'

'You have been wronged?' I teased. 'While you yourself have always been so selfless!'

'Ingratitude is the wages of selflessness.'

'Are you trying to tell me that you are that unique specimen, a man who gives and gives without receiving?'

'I give without expectation.'

'Indeed, what can you expect as long as you withhold the most important thing?'

'I give enough. I am very generous with my favours.'

'I'm glad to hear it. But perhaps we women would rather wait until you give us the gift of your self.'

'I know better. I have learnt that. I have always been the victim of feminine guile.'

'Always?'

'Always.'

'From every woman?'

'Without exception.'

'You have a strange way of giving compliments, monsieur.

No doubt you suspect me as well. So when you invite me to put your love to the test, you are actually asking me to deceive you.'

'Every game becomes more exciting when both players are familiar with the rules.'

'You cynic! Hasn't anyone ever loved you for yourself?'

He had moved closer and now, while considering his answer, he looked into my eyes as if he could see right through my veil. It frightened me.

'I thought so,' he said. I could feel his breath. 'Long ago . . .'

'And?'

'. . . I was deceived.'

He stood there looking miserable, but I saw right through him.

'Very clever, chevalier. But I am smarter. This whole story is to arouse my pity, isn't it?'

'Then at least it would have served some purpose.' He hung his head and looked at me through his lashes like a retriever that has fetched the game and is waiting for its reward.

'One big charade,' I scolded, 'to make me feel an urge to console you. Hats off! You almost succeeded. I did feel a momentary impulse to prove that I am that one trustworthy woman. I have to admit it, you are almost convincing. How many women has that trick worked on?'

'I've lost count.'

'We are worthy opponents,' I laughed.

'Then surely you must have once been disappointed in the same way?'

I remained silent.

'And your story must have won many a man's heart.'

'Your life is a comedy, monsieur. Your little sorrows are merely entr'actes. My drama is a touch more serious. A man

31

can turn his setbacks to his advantage. Life always gives him another chance. For a woman, every blow is absolute.'

'Go on then, speak. Let your story be a lesson to me.'

'Out of the question. No living soul has ever heard my story.'

'Tell it for the first time then to someone who loves you.'

'I will, definitely. The day that someone loves me unconditionally, I will reveal it.'

'I shall do my best to be worthy of such trust.'

'Then you will be disappointed again.'

'The picture you have of men is unforgiving.'

'As is your picture of women. That doesn't deter you from trying to win them.'

At that moment a cry went up outside our window. Immediately afterwards, something thudded onto the ground and we heard the splintering of wood. Seingalt ran out, I followed. A gust of wind had picked up one of the carriages and smashed it against the wall of the bakehouse. The coachman, who had been inside it, sheltering from the rain, was now lying on the ground under one of the shafts. He screamed for help. We were the first to reach him. He was badly injured. The wood had splintered and gouged into his leg, tearing open a long wound. The blood pumped out freely from the large arteries that had been laid bare. I lifted my skirts and tore off three thick strips of fabric. I ordered the chevalier to press the flesh together as hard as he could. He hesitated. My behaviour seemed to astonish him. Evidently he had taken me for one of those women who are too refined for real life. I bandaged the wound so tightly that the bleeding stopped, and then removed as many of the splinters as possible. Finally the unfortunate man was carried off and someone went to fetch a doctor.

Now that the driver seemed to have been saved, I became aware – as one does – of the fright I had suffered. I trembled. For a moment Seingalt and I stood there alone in the night.

He embraced me. I allowed it. He complimented me. Then the horses, which were hitched to a rail, reared as if they felt impending disaster, and a second later a new squall was tugging at the branches and roofs. My dress swelled like a sail. I lost my footing and was dragged several yards across the ground. Seingalt tried to save me, but joined me instead. We ended up sprawled in the mud and couldn't help but burst out laughing. Seingalt's blond wig slipped down almost over his eyes. He took it off.

Beneath it, he had short black curls.

His eyes glinted in the light of a lantern.

Between them was the sharp silhouette of his nose.

A gust of wind took my breath away. I gasped.

'You don't believe that a man can really care for you,' he said, leaning up against me and brushing my shoulder with his cheek. He was seasoned in the art and knew exactly when to make his move. 'Obviously you have never known one who was worthy of your love.'

'Obviously.'

'It is incumbent on me to be the first.'

'Please don't bother.'

I stood up and went inside without his assistance. I excused myself by saying that I needed to clean up a little. In reality I took my cloak and descended to the kitchen, where the coachmen had gathered. None of them dared to take me back to Amsterdam. My departure could not, however, be postponed any longer. I walked to the stables and chose a strong stallion. The groom refused to saddle it, saying that he did not dare to risk his animals on a night like this. But I have braved worse storms. I jumped up onto the horse and spurred it on. I rode it the way I learnt to ride at Pasiano, holding tight to the mane.

It was ungodly along the Amstel. The waves broke over the path. Seven people died that night. But the moon was full. The clouds raced across the sky. I came through it

4

There was another year when everything changed.

In the spring of '42, the Countess of Montereale came to Pasiano earlier than usual. In the very first week of April we were asked to prepare the house, and when she arrived from Venice she brought a complete retinue of artists and workmen with her. The permanent staff of Pasiano were summoned and told that we would spend the whole summer working under the command of the Venetians. They immediately started ordering us about. We had to take down the drapes and the paintings, lower the chandeliers and roll up the carpets. The woodwork was repainted and the walls were lined with embroidered silk. The ponds were drained. The basins were scraped clean, painted light blue and filled with clear water. Two new fountains were installed and small shrubs were planted on the lawn in the precise lines demanded by the latest French fashion. Once the citrus trees had been transplanted into new tubs, work began on transforming the orangery into a reception hall.

The countess was very busy. She rarely left her chambers

and my first attempts to see my 'aunt' failed. Two secretaries I had never seen before refused point-blank to admit me. One morning I had had enough. I took the breakfast tray from her lady's maid, entered her bedroom without knocking, jumped onto her bed and woke her with big kisses. It took her a moment to recover, but when she had, she was delighted to see me and finally explained what all the commotion was about.

Adriana de Montereale had made an excellent match. All the care, time and money that had been invested to improve her position in the marriage market would bear fruit that autumn. The wedding, which would admit her to the Venetian nobility, was to be held in September, and the countess planned to celebrate it by providing the couple with a reception at Pasiano that would be as magnificent as any party held on the Grand Canal.

Explaining all this, the countess seemed tense and not at all happy. She described it more as a trial than a festivity. The mere thought of the work that needed to be done in the coming months to compete with her Venetian acquaintances brought tears to her eyes. I pushed her back down onto her pillows, rubbed her temples and told her that I was surprised that a woman of her wisdom and tranquillity could get herself into such a fluster just to satisfy the whims of the city.

'Ah, child,' she sighed, enjoying the massage. I felt her skin relax beneath my fingers. 'You are good and simple. Thank God you live here and not in Venice. You can't imagine how malicious the people there can be.'

'In Venice?' I couldn't believe my ears. 'Where everyone is so happy?'

'The amount of envy, you have no idea, and the wealthier the people, the worse it gets. Everything comes down to prestige. The men acquire their jobs and status at the assemblies, but that's only half the battle. Their power depends on their reputation. And that's decided by the way others talk about them in the so-called cultured circles. This is where the women enter the lists.

'The ballrooms of Venice are a war zone. Every drawing room is a hostile bay into which one should sail with great caution. One dances, drinks and loves, but meanwhile a battle is raging. The victor rules over the social circuit for a season. In that period, one can safeguard one's future by surrounding oneself with the right people. To achieve that, people fight mercilessly. All means are justified. There is only one rule: everything comes down to appearances. Beauty is the arena in which the women vie with each other.'

She continued in this vein while I massaged her. I thought she was exaggerating and, more importantly, I didn't see the problem. I was free. No one had ever judged me. I didn't really know what it meant. Plus: I was fourteen, an age when a well-built young man is much more appealing than a beanpole. Differentiation based on appearance only seemed healthy. My reaction must have been too frivolous and light-hearted, because the countess sat up and seized my hands, as if suddenly frightened.

'You have no idea how cruel it can be,' she said, resting my hands on her shoulders. For a moment it felt like I was the oldest and she, a girl seeking my protection. 'Yes, everything glitters at those parties, gleaming and sparkling like the treasures under the domes of San Marco. You can't tell from the gold, enamel and porphyry decorating those sacred walls how much blood was spilt plundering the cities of the Levant to acquire them, and it's just as easy to forget that every laugh pealing through the halls of the *palazzi* was won with sweat and tears; that receiving or not receiving an invitation to the right soirée can make or destroy a reputation – what am I saying? It can destroy a *life*! Last season we had to bear the sight of a son of the . . . Actually, I have promised myself that that name will never cross my lips again, but take it from me, it was one of the leading families. Anyway, the poor boy had found the love of his life. She could have been a picture of a girl, really – no one denied that – if only she hadn't had a birthmark, a horrid, purplish-red thing that extended so far up her throat that even the highest of collars couldn't hide it. As soon as their engagement became known, tongues started wagging. The post that had been promised to the young man, as ambassador to Cyprus, went to someone else, from what I heard, merely because his fiancée was considered unsuitable to represent the Serenissima. Because of that birthmark, and for no other reason, his father denied the young couple their happiness. That same night they sailed out into the lagoon together and drowned themselves in the swamp beyond Mazzorbo.'

She fell silent. I screwed my eyes shut as if the poor unfortunates might float up to the surface in the corner of the room.

I shuddered. 'Why on earth would someone give up their life just for love?'

'But, sweetheart, why else?' She looked at me with surprise. 'For heaven's sake, what other reason could there be?' Then she remembered how young I was and kissed me on the forehead, hushing me the way people calm a lapdog.

'I have prayed, every day, and I am still praying that Adriana might make it to her wedding day intact. I've had Masses said. And now it seems, yes, now it really does seem as though . . .'

'But why subject her to all that?' I asked. I had never heard of these things and didn't understand how crucial they were in those circles. 'Adriana could have grown up here, at Pasiano, where we have nothing to fear? I don't understand. If Venice is such a nest of vipers, why do you go back there every winter?'

'Yes,' she said quietly, 'why? Why indeed? One can choose to become a recluse in the country, but that takes so much courage.'

I laughed because I couldn't imagine anywhere safer than Pasiano, but the countess insisted.

'Turning down a path that no one else follows, that requires more strength than I have been able to muster in this life.'

I dressed her. Then I went off to help around the house, but for a long time I found it difficult to derive any pleasure from the preparations.

This grew easier as the festivities approached. At the start of August, suppliers brought cases of wine from Champagne and the island of Madeira. Every evening new musicians dropped by, playing their repertoire by way of audition while we lay in the fields to recover from all our hard work. Two weeks later saw the arrival of a battalion of cooks, cases full of silverware, and the Chinese porcelain the family used in Venice. Seamstresses came to measure the domestic staff for new uniforms.

Towards the end of the month, Adriana arrived with her teacher, Monsieur de Pompignac. While she strode from the carriage to the steps, the Frenchman scuttled around her nervously as though trying to add the last touches of civilisation before delivering his creation to her ancestral home.

Old Count Antonio came from Milan soon after. I had seen him several times before, but on those occasions he had never noticed me. Instead of sharing the countess's rooms, he took up residence in the opposite wing. One afternoon he summoned me there and took me on his lap. He wouldn't stop grinning at me, and I left as soon as I could. That same day, five new coaches were delivered, each with a team of thoroughbreds, to transport the guests. The courier, L'Aigle, a handsome young man, arrived with fourteen large hams from Parma. Someone came from L'Aquila with saffron, and a Slovenian brought chalk for the rhubarb. Every morning you heard the death cries of animals being slaughtered at the surrounding farms. Around midday the carcasses arrived in the kitchen. My mother made sure that the best cuts were properly salted and preserved, and minced the scraps for pastries. My father led an expedition to the mountaintop near Zoldo, between Cadore and Ampezzo. At this time of year he and his men had to climb to great heights, but in the end they brought back so much ice that, even after the cellars had been filled, there was still a pile of snow behind the stables that refused to melt. On hot days the grooms went there to cool off. They made a slope just for me and couldn't get enough of watching me climb up onto it in my chemise and skirt, and slide down on a wooden plank.

Without a worry in the world, I enjoyed all the activity. I couldn't remember having so much fun since the year the fair came to Conegliano. In this way my beloved Pasiano ensured that those months would leave an indelible impression on me, as if it knew that this would be my last carefree summer.

But the high point of my happiness was yet to come. It arrived in the first week of September on a farmer's cart and was almost lost between the ornate carriages that had been coming and going all day long. I was watching all this grandeur from a hidden vantage point between the kitchen and the outbuildings when two youths caught my eye by jumping off the back of a cart outside the gate. They slipped a few soldi to the farmer who had brought them, brushed the oats off their clothes and strolled into the forecourt as if they had just stepped out of a gilded carriage. My laughter was obviously loud enough for them to hear, because one pointed me out and nudged the other, who doffed his hat. For me. His hat! He raised his hat, held it up for a moment and nodded slightly, keeping his eyes fixed on me the whole time. I have enjoyed many courtesies since then, but on my deathbed only this one will appear before me. It was the first time someone had shown me that kind of respect. It was something I had never sought, but now that I had experienced it, I couldn't understand how it was possible that I had never missed it. I wondered whether anyone had ever actually noticed me before. At that same instant, the youth burst out laughing as well. He put a finger to his lips to beg me to secrecy about their poverty and winked to seal our status as co-conspirators.

As bold as brass, the two of them stepped up to my father and gave him their names. They were obviously on the guest list because he ticked something and welcomed them, just as he had done with the others. A servant led them into the salon, where there were snacks and cold drinks for them to enjoy until it was time to show them to their rooms. As soon as my new friends had disappeared into the house, I ran over to my father and tried to read his list to discover who they were. He guessed my thoughts.

'Student priests,' he teased, but in the end he gave me their names: Francesco and Giacomo Casanova. My father accompanied the latter name with an exaggerated impersonation of the gesture with the hat, something he had obviously noticed. Insulted about not being taken seriously, I turned on my heel and went off to look for my mother. I found her in the basement, allocating the rooms. She was standing in the main corridor in front of the large board where the keys to the different rooms were hung on hooks. She crossed off the guests' names on her list as they arrived. Then she jotted the name down on a piece of paper and hung it up next to the number of the room the countess had reserved. Her estimation of my new friends was clearly less lofty than their own, because she had tucked them away in the furthest recesses of the house, three floors up. My heart sank. I never usually went up there anyway, but now that I, along with the rest of the staff's children, had been strictly banned from setting foot in the house for the duration of the festivities, the attic was completely inaccessible.

At that same moment my mother was informed that the Canon of Treviso had arrived. She crossed his name off on her list and wrote it down on a piece of paper. A suite on the first floor had been reserved for him alone, but my mother thought that was a waste for a single man. She paused to think whether there wasn't a smaller alternative that still matched his station. I suggested the room on the east facing the garden. It had a single bed and a beautiful view, and doors that opened onto a terrace not thirty yards from our own cottage . . .

Someone came up to announce the arrival of the next guest.

My mother's head was spinning.

I offered to hang the note with the canon's name next to the right key.

My friend Giacomo was no doubt overjoyed when they showed him his room early that evening. He might have been disappointed to be parted from his brother Francesco, who now had to share the attic with the canon, but Giacomo would have forgotten him soon enough when he realised his neighbours were Venetian aristocrats. At any rate, he threw open the terrace doors with a delighted flourish and took in his surroundings with satisfaction. I thought that he might have been looking for me to play or talk a little, but before I could emerge from the shrubbery where I had been waiting, he had already turned his back. He broke into a run, yelled 'Tally-ho' and leapt onto the bed, where he remained until dinnertime. I didn't want to disturb him and contented myself with the thought that he would soon find the bunch of lavender I had laid under his pillow.

Early the next morning I found the terrace doors to his room ajar. I stepped in through the rippling curtains. Giacomo woke up when I put the tray down on his table. I poured his chocolate and pointed out the dish with fruit jelly. I had picked the red currants myself at my aunt's in Belluno, but thought it would be going too far to say so. I gave him his brioche. He dunked it in the chocolate and took a bite.

He didn't say a word.

I just stood there.

Waiting.

Maybe his eyes needed to adjust to the light.

I had expected him to recognise me from the previous afternoon, but all he did was eat and drink and look at me. Whenever the sheet slid down from his chest, he pulled it up to his chin, as if my standing there embarrassed him.

'Is your bed satisfactory?' I asked at last.

'Absolutely,' he said. 'Did you make it up?'

I nodded. Then we were silent again.

Suddenly I became aware of how I must have looked in his eyes. I was barefoot. I was wearing a chemise, as always, and a skirt. Without daring to take my eyes off him, I felt the waist. I'd buttoned it crooked.

'Who are you?' he asked.

'Lucia!' I couldn't help but sound a little huffy. 'The housekeeper's daughter!' And to make up for that, I immediately rattled off, 'I don't have any brothers or sisters and I'm fourteen.'

'Fourteen,' he said. 'Fine.' He blushed. 'That's good to know.'

'I'm glad you don't have a man-servant. I'll serve you myself. I'm sure you'll be satisfied.'

'I don't doubt it.'

His awkwardness annoyed me. I couldn't understand how someone who had been so bold one day could be so shy the next. I didn't want to stay standing there like that. But I didn't want to give up either. Instead I did the first thing that

43

popped into my head and sat down on the end of his bed. He was so startled that he jerked his legs up. The sheet fell down and left him almost naked. The fright with which he grabbed it and hid behind it with his knees up gave me the giggles.

At the same time I knew that what was happening was of great importance to my life. I didn't know the words for it, but somehow I remembered it. That's what it felt like. It was new, yet instantly familiar. As if something I had actually known since my birth had suddenly occurred to me. What I realised in that instant was that *I* was the one who had robbed Giacomo of his courage. I realised that we could never be friends in the way I had always had friends up till then. There was something between us that kept us apart just as it drew us together. It was the first time I had ever felt that. But I also realised that it was irreversible. That I would never again be able simply to play with all and sundry. This pained and pleased me in equal measure.

Finally he started giggling too. The ice was broken. I passed him his dressing gown and sat awhile on his bed. When my parents came in, they apologised for my behaviour. To my horror, they told Giacomo that I was as virtuous and pure as an angel. My candour and informality were entirely due to my innocence; I was still a child and certain aspects of adulthood were completely unknown to me. They meant well, but I didn't want to hear it. I was overcome by embarrassment. They might just as well have told him that I washed every morning in pigswill. My parents chastised me lovingly, but didn't explain what was inappropriate about my behaviour. I left to get dressed because I could see that that was what they wanted, although I couldn't imagine why. At least Giacomo didn't hold it against me, as I discovered later when I overheard him discussing me with Francesco in the rose garden.

'She's beautiful. She's obedient. She's pious. She's a picture of health. She has white skin and black eyes.'

'This Lucia sounds perfect!'

'You'd think so,' Giacomo said, suddenly gloomy. 'She would be perfect, except for one thing.'

'And that is?'

'She's too young.'

He was serious, but his brother could only laugh. 'A great imperfection!'

5

My mad ride along the Amstel clarified many things. The rain made old sores swell within me. Forgotten scars contracted in the cold. The danger kept me alert. I saw the path I needed to take and all of its pitfalls. Gleaming in the distance were the beacons of Amsterdam. For years I had thought of that city as my final destination. Suddenly, that night, I realised that my journey was not yet over.

Each breath we take, all our dreams, every birth and every death elude our powers of comprehension. Of all our failings, this bothers us the most. Our lives are determined by cosmic processes beyond our grasp. They terrify us and we long for some way of exerting influence over them.

This is magic.

This is what the alchemists are searching for.

They strive to be able to transform things. They write *Know thyself!* on their mirrors and set to work. With burners and retorts, they try to use one substance to turn another into the next. I know nothing about alchemy, but I can tell you this: they have taken the wrong path.

The tangible can only be shaped by the intangible.

The only thing that can change reality is the mind. I have discovered that. To change things, you don't need to touch them, you only need to see them differently. It's nothing. They just need to catch the light for a moment, that's all, like the engraving on the back of the glass. Suddenly you've seen it and can hardly believe you never noticed it before.

This is the elusive cosmic process.

I know it.

I have experienced it.

Call it love and I am a magician.

Once the storm had died down, I set to work. It was a question of change or be changed. I sent the chevalier an apology for my overhasty departure and suggested that we pursue our acquaintance. An answer did not come at once as he had gone to The Hague on business, but on the last day of the month I received news that the Chevalier de Seingalt had taken up residence nearby in the Doelenstraat. I informed him that I was expecting him at my home and added, for the sake of clarity, that Holland is more liberal than the rest of Europe. Dutch women are brought up fully aware of the dangers that beset them and are taught to behave accordingly. As a consequence, people see no harm at all in women entertaining unchaperoned guests.

He presented himself that same evening. Although it was obvious that he had not been expecting such a modest flat, he still treated me with all due respect. Not a word betrayed his surprise at the conditions under which I lived. His conversation was somewhat milder than it had been at our previous encounter, but I attributed that to a growing familiarity. Despite everything, I too felt more at ease. I had asked the cook of the Cow's Head to prepare a small dinner for us. When it was brought to the house, Seingalt insisted on settling the account with the delivery boy. He did this so quickly and naturally that I did not feel the slightest awkwardness.

His approach was more cautious this time as well. His tone was just as playful and amorous, but he no longer insisted on any disclosures. The humbleness of my possessions formed such a sharp contrast to my appearance that he was in no hurry to enquire about my adventures. I took the opportunity to question him about his.

'Do you think the years have changed you?' I asked eventually.

'Not years, but people.'

'And how did they manage that?'

'By showing me how superficial they are.'

'So you could imagine yourself to be smarter.'

I poured some wine. It smelt tart, but that didn't seem to bother him.

'You don't need to be very clever to outsmart people,' he continued. 'They want to be deceived. You get further by being brazen. No, I changed because I lost my respect.'

'For them?'

'And partly for myself, too, as a result. I don't deny that I took advantage of their gullibility. I had no compunction about cheating dunces, rogues and nincompoops whenever it seemed necessary.'

He clearly took pleasure in his own villainy. Grinning, he recounted several deceptions he had practised in all corners of Europe.

It is true that people stand in line to be swindled. I, too, have turned that to my advantage often enough. The rapid development of science in our century has torn people apart from within. The simple-minded – and I was once one of them – do not doubt what they feel. Their only concern is the things that influence their day-to-day life. They respond to these things impulsively, as they have for generation upon generation, and anything they can't resolve with this approach they leave in the hands of a Supreme Being. The new discoveries, however, contradict these emotions; even the existence of God is no longer a certainty. Many of the people who immerse themselves in these matters have grown confused. They do not yet dare to put all of their trust in reason and they are still unable fully to relinquish their faith. They remind me of a hunter I once saw on the river. He had ventured out onto the ice too late in the season and was floating downstream with his feet on two different floes. He couldn't decide which one to step onto and drowned. Many of our new thinkers are adrift in the same way. They try to anchor themselves on two banks at once: reason and emotion. They try to use science to find proof of a spiritual life. This is the key to the success that magicians and alchemists enjoy among educated people. They claim to be enlightened by reason, but follow these will-o'-the-wisps.

Meanwhile Seingalt gave a practised account of various simpletons whose folly he had saluted by using their own delusions to swindle them. He seemed accustomed to reaping success with these burlesque anecdotes, but I was interested in the man himself, not his knavish tricks, and cut him short.

'Don't you agree,' I ventured, 'that it is, when travelling, seductively simple to adopt a new guise?' He looked at me for a moment, but did not dare to ask what I was alluding to or how I had come to this knowledge. For a moment I was afraid that I had been too forthright and had aroused his suspicions. 'For me, at least, it has always been a tremendous comfort,' I added, 'to know that in the future one can leave everything behind and – if necessary – slough off one's own existence, literally, like a snake that sheds its skin between two stones.'

'It's true, whenever you arrive somewhere new you can pretend to be someone else. No one knows you, and everyone is keen to fit you into some kind of category. That's a human need; people are more than willing to believe whatever you tell them. And if they require proof, a simple letter of recommendation with an impressive name on it will do the trick. Theoretically, it's quite possible to be a physician in one country, an opera singer in the next and a lawyer three days down the road.'

'And you want us in Holland to believe that the government of France has sent you to the Amsterdam bourse as a banker?' I teased. 'You must have an especially low estimation of our intelligence not to have come up with something a little more plausible.'

'Fortunately I have as evidence bills of exchange from the bank worth twenty million francs . . .'

'Please don't bother, monsieur. As I don't have a sou to pledge, financial matters are of no interest to me. You have my blessing. But I do not like to be deceived. I can tell you that now. Your name, for instance, is French, but your accent reveals quite different origins.'

He admitted it and told me his real name. I listened impassively. He explained that he had only recently exchanged his Italian identity for a French one that was more consistent with his employment by the state.

'Being neither important nor influential is a blessing in disguise,' I said, 'otherwise I might fear that your behaviour towards me bore little relation to your actual self.'

'As if winning you were not important to me!'

'Then rest assured that I can only be won by the truth. All others die before the gates.'

He burst out laughing.

'There *is* another truth.'

'I suspected as much,' I said. 'There always is.'

'Perhaps you prefer this one . . .'

Whereupon he dished up an insane story about an elderly Parisienne, a certain Madame d'Urfé, who had succumbed to occult delusions and believed herself in possession of the philosopher's stone. She had become so enchanted by Seingalt's arts that she cherished the hope that he would be able to resurrect her soul in a male body after her death. To acquire the apparatus necessary for this procedure, she had asked him to sell, in Amsterdam, all of her shares in the Dutch East India Company.

He stared at me shamelessly.

'Every last word of that is true,' he said, 'but does it sound any more plausible? Do you see now why I call it folly to be too attached to the truth, when a dash of fantasy is so much easier to believe?'

'Touché,' I admitted wholeheartedly, 'you're right, reality is generally more peculiar than anything people can invent.' Life had taught me that, and Seingalt's presence in my flat was the living proof. 'In any case,' I resumed, 'once more I can add a name to the long list of women you have deceived. Poor Madame d'Urfé.'

'As far as women are concerned: the deception is mutual and doesn't count; when love is involved, both parties are duped. And as for Madame d'Urfé: it is different when one is dealing with fools. They know no shame and their conceit is beyond description. The man who cheats a fool is avenging reason.'

'She doesn't believe that you love her?'

'No, she thinks I am a sorcerer.'

'And are you?'

'Certainly, for those who want me to be.'

I laughed. That seemed to gall him.

'I do not toy with their confidence, madame. I definitely don't want you to think that,' he said seriously. 'There's nothing strange about people taking me for someone who can help them. Over the years I have become proficient in many useful fields, such as chemistry, which enables me to carry out impressive experiments, and cryptography, which allows me to decode the most intricate of formulae. For my own personal improvement, I have also studied the cabbala and the works of Lull and Hermes Trismegistus.'

'You leave nothing to chance with your deceptions.'

'I have amassed my knowledge purely for my own benefit – you will have to take my word for that. Motivated by genuine interest alone. If others can turn it to their advantage as well, all the better.'

'Most noble,' I sneered.

'As a virtue, I have always considered nobility quite overrated. I have never professed to be part of humanity's just minority. I don't encourage anyone to believe in me, but in this day and age there just happen to be large numbers of people who are desperately in search of security. I don't take that lightly. I owe my own life to the fact that I once believed someone who hoodwinked me. I was eight years old . . .' His voice sounded gentler than it had during his previous stories. He searched for words among the images he himself was evoking. '. . . eight years old. One evening I stood up in my room. I was looking down. Blood was dripping on the tiles. I counted the drops and tried to follow their fall with my eyes. Suddenly I realised that it was my own blood. It was pouring out of my nose – I remember it vividly. I stood in the corner by the window and called my grandmother. She washed my face with cold water. When she saw how serious it was, she took me to a shack outside the city. An old woman lived there. She was sitting on a bed with a black cat in her arms. She was a witch. My grandmother gave her some money. Then the witch put me in a chest. By that time I had lost so much blood I was dizzy. I was too far gone to be scared and just lay there with a rag pressed against my nose, listening to the noises I could hear around me. There was singing, shouting, laughter and crying, and regular blows against the chest. Finally the witch pulled me out again. The bleeding had stopped. She hugged me, undressed me and laid me on the bed. Then she burnt some herbs, caught the smoke in a sheet and wrapped me up in it. She gave me five delicious sweets. The bleeding would stop, she said, as long as I never told anyone about that night, but if I betrayed a single word of what had happened, my veins would empty themselves and I would die. Then she let me go with the promise that I would be visited that same night by an enchanting, beautiful lady on whom my happiness would depend. And so it was. The lady appeared towards morning. I saw – or thought I saw, that's irrelevant – a dazzling beauty emerge from the fireplace. The woman was wearing a glittering, jewel-studded crown and a magnificent dress with a wide hoop. She gave a long speech of which I understood not a word, kissed me and left the way she had come.'

He looked at me as if he were surprised that I had let him finish the story without interruption.

'Then I fell asleep,' he added. He had lowered his voice, almost to a whisper. He took my hand. Through my veil he could not possibly see the effect his story had had on me, but he suspected it and wanted to reassure me.

Never have I known a man who could empathise so well with a woman.

'The cures for serious illnesses are not always found in a pharmacy,' he said, 'that is something I have realised thoroughly since then. That is why I never trifle with the faith people put in me, because once someone has given you her trust, a mere suggestion can be enough to devastate or heal.'

At this point, I was no longer able to control myself and began to sob with great heaves of my chest. He was shocked and could not possibly have suspected why this one, of all his tall stories, should have touched me like this. He sat there like a little boy who doesn't know what to do.

'Many things that exist only in the imagination,' he said, 'later become real . . .'

I tried with all my might to catch my breath and calm

down so that I could stop him from going on, but it was too much for me. The possible effects of every word I might now speak raced through my mind. It was too frightening. I couldn't foresee the consequences. I didn't know how to respond and every word I thought of seemed dangerous. All I could come up with was to clench my teeth and sit as still as possible, not even wiping my cheeks, anything to make him think that my sorrowful outburst had been a passing whim.

'. . . and the evidence of that was provided again eight years later, when I recognised the beauty who visited me when I was a child in the face of my very first love.'

'How lovely,' I said finally. My annoyance that he would use such nonsense to win me helped me regain my composure. 'Falling in love with a face one thinks one remembers from a dream, I find *that* rather superficial.'

This response threw him off-balance. He began to defend himself. He was probably used to this tender song melting women's hearts so completely that they immediately suspended all resistance. I, in the meantime, had begun to suspect that every move he made was strategic and subservient to conquest.

'If your love goes no deeper than a face you remember because you happened to have dreamt it, it's hardly flattering for the girl in question. Didn't she have any qualities of her own?'

'I never meant it that way, I just . . .'

'Why did you love her then?'

'How am I supposed to remember that? You ask about my first love and many have come and gone since then.'

'No doubt,' I said. 'Perhaps I should ask what she saw in you, that's something men generally remember better.'

After this we spoke of other things for a while, but the friendly atmosphere was gone. I made it obvious that his visit was drawing to a close with his goal still unachieved. It had grown late as well, and I was expecting Giovanna and Danae to arrive at any moment to hand over their earnings. By the end of the night the Parmesans could look very tired, used and sleazy. Not wanting to subject the chevalier to their slatternliness, I said goodbye and showed him to the door. He was already in the street when something occurred to him and he turned back to face me.

'I loved my first love because she poured me a glass of water.'

'Water as the basis for love?' I joked. 'And you were surprised it didn't last?'

'One day she poured me some water. It was an ordinary glass, but she held it up to the light as if it were a crystal chalice. I looked, but no matter how I tried, I couldn't see what she saw in it. "Water takes on the shape of the vessel." Her voice was full of awe. "Just now it was the shape of the jug, now it's the shape of the glass." She said it as if she were drawing my attention to a wonder. I laughed at her. Shocked, she looked up. Tears leapt to her eyes. "It seemed such a miracle. It always surprised me. The water in the stream is shaped like the banks. In my hands it takes on the shape of my palms." She really was quite distraught. "I thought it was so special. I wanted to share it with you. And now you think I'm silly." I did my best to deny it, but she was inconsolable. "It's not that," she sobbed. "It's just . . . I always thought it so beautiful and from now on it will just be ordinary." '

Monsieur le Chevalier de Seingalt was still standing in the street with his hat in his hand. It was raining, but he didn't seem to have noticed. His eyes were still trying to find mine through my veil.

'Why should a miracle not be a miracle just because someone else can't see it?'

6

My parents got on well with Giacomo. They were still
talking to him when I re-entered his room. I had washed in
the meantime and put up my hair. I was wearing a clean dress
and I had put on some shoes, something I wasn't used to.

'Is that better?'

I turned around and reaped their applause. Giacomo
patted his bedspread as a sign that I was now welcome to
come and sit on his bed.

'Dressed and all?' I said haughtily. 'No, sir, it's all well and
good as long as you don't think about it, but sitting down on
a bed in my best clothes, no, that's too grand for me.'

My answer seemed to please everyone.

'She's a lot nicer like this than in her chemise, isn't she?'
asked my mother. The young *abbé* looked me over from
head to toe and I could tell that he didn't agree. When a
footman arrived to do his hair, we left him alone. Later that
day, when I made his bed, I left a vase with fresh flowers on
the table with a small brass bell.

★

The next morning he rang for his breakfast. I delivered it to him the way he liked to see me. I was much surer of myself than I had been the day before and climbed onto the foot of his bed. We talked like that for quite a while. He seemed more at ease as well, and when I rolled over onto my stomach to listen to him with my head on my hands, he came and lay down beside me. He told me that he had studied law in Padua and had recently graduated, just before his seventeenth birthday. As if that wasn't enough, the patriarch of Venice himself had already tonsured the prodigy and conferred the minor orders on him.

When I asked whether he was planning to enter a monastery, he answered by blowing into my chemise so that it billowed out and gave him a better view. I lashed out at him and we wrestled until we were out of breath. That was all. Then we lay side by side for a while until we recovered.

I told him about my grandfather and the mirrors in the grand salon. Suddenly I felt his hand on my breast. I was startled and moved back, but the hand followed. I was not yet fully developed. I was aware of that, but never so painfully. There was no doubt in my mind that I must have disappointed him. I blushed. I could already hear how different his conversation with his brother Francesco would be today. In a matter of seconds, I imagined every word of their exchange, including their howls of derision among the rose bushes. My cheerfulness fled. I grew so confused that Giacomo finally released me. I immediately regretted my actions. What would he think of me? Now I really felt embarrassed. To make amends, I moved closer. I took his hand and told him that I hadn't meant to be unfriendly. He reassured me.

'You are innocent,' he said, as if that were news. 'It's just that you're free and not prim at all. You have no idea how confusing a certain relaxed attitude you don't mean anything by can be for a young man.'

He ate the rolls I sugared for him while telling him about the animals in the fields and the overseer's dogs and my adventures in the forests around Pasiano. He interrupted me in mid-sentence, as if he hadn't been listening, to ask if I was cold and whether I wouldn't be warmer if I crawled in under the blankets beside him.

'Wouldn't that be difficult for you?'

'Not at all, I'm just scared your mother might come in.'

'She wouldn't think badly of it.'

'But you know the risk we're taking?'

'I'm not stupid. And you're sensible. And a priest.'

I snuggled up next to him and continued my story, but it was like he was deaf. He couldn't concentrate on a word I was saying and I soon grew tired of talking to a wall. It was already ten o'clock and I told him that I wanted to get up because Count Antonio sometimes crossed the terrace at that time of the morning and I wanted to avoid him at any cost.

'I'm leaving now,' I said when Giacomo insisted that I stay to help him get dressed, 'because I have no curiosity at all about seeing you upright.' He groaned.

Later that day he apparently had a conversation with my parents, who told me about it much later. He said that he was convinced that I was an angel incarnate who could not fail to fall victim to the first womaniser she encountered. He promised them that it would not be him and that he had resolved to control himself. He meant it! My parents, grown anxious, could think of no one they would rather see safeguard my honour. They asked whether the young priest could cultivate my mind and take me under his wing in the days ahead. And whether he might, while maintaining my innocence, inform me of the dangers of youth.

When my mother walked into his room from the garden the next day, she seemed perfectly content to find me on the bed. She was so happy she even kissed me, telling me that I was the consolation of their love and old age, and thanking Giacomo for the moral lessons he was going to give me. The young priest said that it would only be much later that I would realise how lucky I was to have parents who were so open-minded and trusting.

He turned out to be right about that.

From the moment I knew that my parents supported me, I no longer felt awkward in Giacomo's presence. During the week of the festivities, I was in his room every morning. He spent the rest of the day participating in the parties and excursions the countess had arranged. Sometimes I would see him briefly on the terrace in the evening, but generally I had to wait until the next morning, when I threw myself onto his bed and covered his face with kisses.

The week of festivities ended with a large display of fireworks, lit from diverse places in the hills around Pasiano. My father was in charge of the fountains and cascades that were going to be lit close to the wooded bank north of the house. I was there with him and excited about the spectacle that was about to begin.

'Here she goes!' my father cheered while holding the tinder under the first fuse. 'Just say, "Goodbye, dear guests, thanks for nothing and see you never!" '

It was as if that first bang woke me up. The awareness that my playmate would be leaving in the morning with the other guests flared up inside me. I leapt up shrieking. My father was shocked by the violence of my reaction and tried with all his might to restrain me, but he had to make sure that everything was going safely at the same time and I broke free. In a panic, I ran over fields that were lighting up red, yellow and blue around me. Burning debris fell down to the left and right of me, but I didn't care. I raced towards the mansion, lit up in the distance with Bengal light. The guests had gathered at the top of the steps. When they saw me, some yelled to me to take cover, but I refused to listen and ran on through a shower of smouldering stars. At the house I fell down on my knees in front of the countess. Before I could speak, she had already guessed what I was thinking because Giacomo had pushed his way through the crowd and was bending over me solicitously.

'Am I really to be so blessed, my dear,' she laughed, 'as to see history repeat itself?' She exchanged knowing looks with my mother, who had rushed up as well, and I heard Count Antonio make a remark about me. For a second I was annoyed that everyone seemed to have realised what was happening to me before I did. Then the countess asked Giacomo whether he would be so friendly as to stay behind and keep us company at Pasiano for the whole month of September.

We now had plenty of time and I took him to all the corners of my world. We left before dawn to see the deer in Codopé and walked on to Azanello. There we made a fire in the ruins to toast the bread my mother had given us. The rest of the day we wandered through the fields or tried to lure the horses in the meadow near Cornizzai, so that we could climb onto their backs, holding tight to their manes until they bucked and we fell off, screaming with laughter.

These days passed like a dream in which everything seems familiar even though you can't place it. I thought that I had discovered all there was to know about Pasiano in my fourteen years, but now, showing Giacomo around, it was as if I was aware of my home for the first time. Some of the places I had always loved disappointed me now that I saw them as they must have appeared to him. I did my best to explain what I had found so beautiful, but even as I spoke I heard the conviction draining from my words. Other things that I had never really noticed suddenly glowed when they caught his eye. One moment I felt sorrow, as if I had betrayed my old self, the next I was overjoyed because my perspective had been enriched. My world grew because my consciousness was doubled. I felt that very clearly. It was no longer limited to my own thoughts, but suddenly included everything he thought and felt and desired and hoped.

When we were hot in the afternoon, we swam in the lake on the Rivarotta, then lay on the shore to dry. Meanwhile I asked him questions. I wanted to know everything. Sometimes, when he had told me an anecdote, I asked him to tell it to me again, from start to finish, scared that I might have missed a detail or that he could have left something out. And the next afternoon I wanted to hear it all over again.

He seemed to lead an extraordinary life and his adventures made my head spin. At Pasiano people grew old without experiencing a fraction of the things Giacomo had already been through in his seventeen years. Only at the spring fair in Sacile had I once heard something similar, when a street singer sang the adventures of Gil Blas while his assistants depicted them as tableaux.

In his short life, Giacomo had already been to Constantinople and Corfu, and everywhere he went he got into fights and played the hero. It didn't seem possible that one person could have experienced so much. When I heard that his parents were actors, I wondered whether he hadn't just made it up, but he seemed serious. Especially when talking about his mother, Zanetta.

One day he told me how she had abandoned him as a toddler to pursue a career on the stage in London, where she was impregnated by the Prince of Wales. Whatever the truth of it, he became emotional. He loved her and he hated her; that much was clear. His actress mother had sullied the family name and he seemed determined to restore it to its former glory. Giacomo wanted to pursue a career as a diplomat, following in the footsteps of forebears who, in the past three centuries, had served a series of glorious names, of which I remember King Alphonsus II of Spain, Cardinal Pompeo Colonna and Christopher Columbus. He wanted to play an equally important role in history. For the son of two actors, a position with that kind of potential was as good as unattainable, but he had set his mind on it. He had already taken the first steps towards this goal whilst a protegé of the renowned Senator Malipiero, in whose home on the Grand Canal he had grown accustomed to the company of the powerful and illustrious. He spoke of his ambition with a fervour that sometimes scared me because it made him seem utterly ruthless, and sometimes filled me with envy because I myself was unable to feel that passionate about anything at all and might never get further than a workhouse in Pordenone. In a brief moment of clarity, I also felt threatened by his dream, although I couldn't say why.

He spoke about the career before him as if it were a naval battle he could not afford to lose. His preparations had been meticulous and he knew just which positions to take. This winter he would make a number of important allies in Venice and try to obtain an appointment with Venier, the Venetian ambassador to Turkey, whom he knew from Constantinople. While telling me all this, he saw a growing look of dismay on my face. He apologised and said that, of course, it was impossible for me to understand how hard Venetians could be. I disagreed.

'The countess has told me everything about her daughter. I happen to know exactly what sacrifices a woman must undergo in that city. Her life is a constant struggle. And all that, just to find a husband, something that happens naturally in any village you care to pick. I can very well imagine the struggles of a man who has to attain a position there.'

He looked at me sweetly. For the first time since starting to talk about his future, he was once again truly aware of my presence, and I felt a childish relief, like the time the overseer's dog came walking up the path after being missing for a week. Simultaneously, however, I was overwhelmed by an adult desire that submerged all others. 'Yes,' I thought for the first time, 'I want him to succeed. Giacomo has the potential to rise above himself. That has been determined from on high.' I had never been so convinced of anything. In that instant I would have given up everything for him to achieve his goal and be happy.

Then he told me that, when he was a child, his grandmother had taken him to the island of Murano to see a witch who cured his bleeding. In the night that followed he was visited by a fairy, who – so he said – I reminded him of.

Many times during those weeks I asked myself, 'Why is a young man like him wasting his time on someone like me?' Don't misunderstand me: in his presence I felt more beautiful than before or after. I imagined myself smarter than ever, and when I made him laugh I felt vivacious and witty. And yet, 'a girl like me . . .' It seemed too good to be true. Alone in my bed at the end of the day, I was always scared that he would come to his senses that night in his room and reconsider, not even bothering to summon me the following morning. But once I had finally fretted myself to sleep, I sunk back into deep happiness because he had already given me so much.

One morning he rang earlier than usual. It was hardly light. I threw on some clothes. My hair was still down, but I ran to him with open arms, as elated as ever. I stopped in the middle of his room. I was shocked. He looked pale, miserable and upset.

'What's wrong?'

'I couldn't sleep.'

'Why not?'

'There is something I am obliged tell you,' he said. 'It is

terrible to be forced to admit it, but by doing so I shall win your respect.'

'If that prize makes you so wretched, I'd prefer you aim a little lower.' I was worried, but pretended to take it lightly. 'And tell me why you're talking to me as if I'm a lady, when yesterday we were such good friends? What have I done wrong, signor *abbé*? I'll go fetch your breakfast and once you've had it, you'd best tell me the whole story.'

I don't know how I found the kitchen or made it back with a full tray and a jug of hot water. My knees were trembling. I poured his drink and he drank it silently. Meanwhile I tidied his room and closed the door to keep out the draught. Then I got into bed with him and snuggled up close so as not to miss a word. The story he told was quite something. It was filled with arguments he had thought out in advance and it took at least fifteen minutes. I wasn't the kind of person who thought with her head. I didn't believe in it. I only knew what I felt, and I didn't try to follow his line of reasoning. What he called logic, I only knew as folly.

'I'm in love with you.' That was what his argument came down to. 'I love you so much that I can no longer control myself. That is why we mustn't see each other any more.'

What could I say? I stared at him as if he had spoken Arabic.

I am thirsty so I will not drink.

I am hungry so I fast.

In Udine there is a house where they strap people like that down on a wooden bench until they come to their senses.

Nonetheless, Giacomo seemed to know what he was doing. Moved to the point of tears, he described the horrors that awaited us if we continued to see each other. Until then he had managed to control himself by resorting to the special remedy of schoolboys, which he had applied several times a day, but this, he said, had proved insufficient. He was no

65

longer able to vouch for his own behaviour and would never forgive himself if he defiled my honour.

My eagerness to forgive him in advance for that same thing seemed to make no difference. He began to weep. I dried his tears with the front of my chemise, but the view I allowed him by doing so only enlarged his dilemma.

'You love me,' I said, 'and because of that you banish me. I wonder what you would do if you hated me.' I felt like crying now as well, but swallowed my tears. 'You have studied, I'm just a simple girl. Still I'm cleverer than you, because I know that love is not a disease. At least, I know it has made *me* feel better than ever. Until today. I'll do whatever you ask of me, but I can't stop loving you. If the only way of curing you is for us never to see each other again, then so be it. I would rather have you healthy without me than watch you pine away in my presence. But I still can't understand it. Are you sure there's no other solution, because the grief of this one will surely kill me?'

That touched him.

'Nature's arguments are so much stronger than morality's,' he said, taking me in his arms.

'Please,' I whispered, 'think of something. Maybe it's not that exceptional. Think of something else. You can count on Lucia.'

And an alternative remedy immediately occurred to him.

After an hour we were interrupted by my mother, who came to tell me to get dressed for Mass. I was able to leave my patient with a clear conscience, as a healthy colour had already returned to his cheeks.

From then on we kissed each other every day for hours on end and played all the games that mouths can play. I already loved life, but now I also gained a deep and pious respect for its ability to grant us something so divine. We were insatiable, for the very reason that Giacomo restrained himself from that one thing that would have squandered our honour. He alone can take the credit for that. Heaven knows I did everything in my power to undermine his resolution. I even tried telling him that the fruit had already been plucked, whereupon he laid me down for an examination that lasted for ever and drove me wild. He seemed so familiar with femininity that it was impossible to deceive him.

In his hands, I felt completely safe. At the same time I was at the mercy of a searing lust. It must have been during these days that those two emotions merged. The more I opened myself up to my lover, revealing my soul as well as my body, the more certain I was of his protection. Because I dared to trust him, I was able to lose myself completely. For me, lust and security have been interwoven ever since, and this has determined the course of my life. Nothing has ever made me feel more secure than being shameless.

We were still in this heavenly state when the month of October arrived. The countess was returning to Venice and the remaining guests were expected to accompany her.

We were inconsolable.

Giacomo declared his willingness to renounce all of the plans he had made for his future. He had already composed a letter of apology to Senator Malipiero. I tore it up. He offered to remain at Pasiano and earn a living in the fields. I forbade it. This was not self-sacrifice on my part. On the contrary. I have never been able to summon up any admiration for people who allow their minds to decide affairs of the heart. No, I let him go from self-interest. After all, his happiness would mean my happiness, I felt that very clearly. And to be happy, he needed to pursue his dream. I wasn't unhappy. I already had mine.

We agreed that he would return the following spring, as soon as the winter season in Venice was over, so that we could get engaged after Lent. The countess wanted to help us. She asked her husband, who was not feeling well and had temporarily postponed his departure for Milan, to extend Monsieur de Pompignac's appointment. His task completed after the wedding, Adriana's teacher had already packed his bags but was delighted to hear of the extension to his employment. Confident of his abilities, he listened to the task presented to him by the countess, and promised to brush up my knowledge in the coming autumn and winter and quickly teach me the etiquette of high society so that I would be able to fit in as a diplomat's wife. Because we were all agreed: next summer Pasiano would be the scene of another wedding, Giacomo's and mine!

Even on the eve of our farewell, I was unable to seduce the man I had entrusted with my heart and my soul into doing the one thing I still longed for. Instead we wept in each other's arms until morning and promised to remain true to each other in this life and the next.

While waving goodbye to the carriages, I heard the elderly count give a sniff next to me. And again, as if something was on fire somewhere.

'You're nice and ripe,' he said. 'Don't bother denying it, I can smell it. I've learnt that over the years. That briny smell.' He filled his lungs greedily. 'Yes, I can smell when a girl's ready for it.'

I ran through the gate and down the road all the way to Pozzo and further still until they had all disappeared from sight and even the dust had settled.

7

'Why should a miracle not be a miracle just because someone else can't see it?'

The Chevalier de Seingalt was still standing before my door, lost in thought in the cold Dutch drizzle. His wig was getting wet. Dark wet patches appeared on his expensive silk jacket. The memory of the girl who once held up a glass and wondered at the changing shape of water had upset him.

'You know, we even promised to be eternally faithful to each other,' he said suddenly, as if waking from a dream. 'She promised to wait for me, but when I came looking for her, not six months later, she had disappeared.'

'Maybe she had good reason.'

'Indeed she did,' he said, bowing goodbye again. 'She was a woman.'

II

A Great Imperfection

Not far from Pasiano, on the bank of the Livenza, an ancient hermit lived in a wine butt. Sometimes my mother sent me there with a jug of milk or some leftover bread. The old man had spent his whole life fasting and praying, mercilessly flagellating himself and denying himself all worldly pleasures. All in the hope that, just once before he died, he might be able to imitate Christ and perform a miracle by walking on water. This was his only goal, and he practised every day from early in the morning until late at night. In front of his hovel there were always a few habits hung out to dry.

Then, one day, I arrived to find his clothes-line empty. The old man was sitting on the ground in front of his barrel, tucking into roast lamb and a bottle of lambrusco.

'I've done it!' he told me. 'Last night the Saviour appeared to me. He stood right there on the opposite bank and waved for me to come on over. He wanted to see what I had dedicated my whole life to. The moment of truth had arrived and I was nervous. Then I stepped, very carefully, out onto the water, and it worked! I stayed dry. It was a true miracle. I could hardly believe it: one step at a time I reached the middle of the river. Jesus was so happy He clapped His hands! That made me feel braver and with a few big steps I reached Him on the opposite bank. I fell into His arms. "This is what I've given my whole life for," I sobbed, "renouncing all worldly pleasures so that one day I would be able to walk from one side of the river to the other."

'Christ's face clouded over with pity.

'"Oh," said the Saviour, "what a waste! Just a few hundred yards downstream, there's a ferry." '

The world is full of people who spend their entire life searching for the miracle of love without ever seeing it. It is very simple and self-evident, but lost to those who search for it.

All it takes is a different way of seeing things.

That is not something you can teach people. All you can do is tell your story.

up skirt, Monsieur de Pompignac composed himself and informed me that he expected to see me in the library at ten o'clock the next morning. He then asked me to put one of my feet up on the bed. Scarcely able to believe his eyes, he inspected my calluses and left with sagging shoulders.

I wore shoes to that first lesson. They were my mother's and too big for me, but Monsieur de Pompignac appreciated the gesture. He was despairing rather than unfriendly. He paced around me like Madame de Maintenon's hairdresser circling a stray dog. He asked me questions, which I answered to the best of my ability. Now and then he smiled at one of my replies, although none of them seemed to make him any more cheerful. Between questions he told me things that, in their turn, meant nothing to me. Not wanting to disappoint him, I kept a friendly smile on my face. Eventually he fell silent. He led me over to the window, took my face in his hands and turned it so that it caught the light at several different angles. He sighed that at least my cheekbones were acceptable. Then he tried to send me off with the adventures of Gil Blas in four leather-bound volumes, announcing that we would discuss them the next morning. I leafed through them quickly, but gave them back. I could read – that wasn't the problem – but I wasn't very fast and I told him there was no point in my trying to read something with so many difficult words. De Pompignac stared at me open-mouthed. He browsed through one of the books as if to reassure himself that it really was printed in my own language and not in Aramaic. Then he relaxed. Slowly, as the full extent of my ignorance dawned on him, a smile appeared on his face. I was embarrassed and offered apologies he refused to accept.

'My whole life,' he said, 'I have struggled to make something of the debris that others have left behind. Filling gaps, plugging holes, repairing cracks, smoothing off rough edges . . . And now, just when I thought it was all over, for the first time, I have been given a chance to show what I can create from a block of unhewn marble. Mine, all mine, from the first blow of the chisel. It will be hard. It will hurt, of course it will, but what did you expect? Did Pygmalion let that stop him? We will shed tears of blood, but it is now or never!'

I wanted to leave, but he asked me to sit down and began opening books on the table in front of me. I read them the way I thought they should sound. He corrected me and explained exactly what they meant, over and over, until I started to recognise certain phrases and dared to guess at their meaning. We kept at it for hours. I grew hungry and thirsty. He called for water and a piece of almond cake, but wouldn't let me stop long enough to eat it, so I had to gulp it down chunk by chunk while reciting the conjugations he was drilling into me.

When the sun set at the end of that first day we were both exhausted.

That night I didn't sleep.

I read.

Carefully I studied line after line. Then I tried to say them out loud. I remember the surprise I felt when a word that looked like so much mumbo-jumbo on the page took on a familiar sound after I had stuttered it out a few times. Suddenly I realised – and I hesitate to admit it because soon after that I could no longer imagine ever having been so foolish – that all those symbols, even the many I could not yet decipher, simply stood for things I had known for years. This realisation put an end to the fear that books had always inspired in me. And with my fear, I also shrugged off the mocking attitude I had adopted towards the written word and the kind of people who always have their heads in books. The insecurity that had given birth to that mocking was still there, but I had found a new way of dealing with it.

'You can eat cake all your life without ever knowing what's in it,' I thought, 'but you'll always need someone else to make it for you. Once you take the trouble of finding out the ingredients, you'll be able to feed yourself for the rest of your life.'

The next morning I read the first page of *Gil Blas* to Monsieur de Pompignac.

A smile started to spread over his face.

'*Ma Galathée!*' he whispered.

He hauled himself up out of his chair, took my hand and kissed it, something no one had ever done before.

Nobody could have anticipated the success that followed. Studying seemed to suit me. Keen to please my teacher, I exploited this talent to the full and hardly showed my face out of doors – much to the regret of the stableboys and L'Aigle, the courier. (Around this time L'Aigle was thrashed and sent off for molesting a kitchenmaid, something he did in a sulk over my rejecting him.) At night I kept myself awake over my books by thinking about the delight I would see in the eyes of my elderly tutor in the morning. My hunger for learning had been aroused, and I was insatiable. After Count Antonio relieved me of my domestic duties – in exchange for a kiss – I was able to dedicate myself to my lessons all day. At night I couldn't stop. It was as if I felt that I had to use the bare months of this year to harden myself, arming myself with knowledge against all that would follow when the buds reappeared on the trees. My eyes were fixed on the prize that awaited me at the end of my studies. The diploma held out to the students of Bologna could not possibly motivate them as much as I was motivated by the thought of Giacomo's astonishment at recognising me as an intellectual equal when he returned in the spring.

From Lesage, my teacher led me to the adventures of Manon

Lescaut and through the minds of many of the greatest thinkers of our age. They tried to liberate themselves from the slavery of emotion, just as I was trying to rise above my state of nature. Their rule of reason appealed to me. I discovered it together with them and the more I learnt about it, the more I realised how powerful a weapon it was.

Each time he saw his efforts rewarded, Monsieur de Pompignac set his goals higher. In just a few days he began giving his lessons partly in French. My grasp of that language was rudimentary, to say the least, but he claimed that it was the voice of science and the future of Europe and that I would prove intelligent enough to master it. Sure enough, within two weeks I was able to reply to him in more or less his own words, after which we began to read through French works line by line. He brought more and more books for me: Nani's *Histoire de Venise*, Fontenelle's *Mondes* and his *Dialogues des mortes*, Bossuet's treatises on world history and Le Sueur's *Histoire de l'Eglise et de l'Empire*.

Soon his lessons extended to physical exercises designed to improve my posture. He wanted me to sit like a marionette that is being held up by a single string attached to its chest and he insisted that I always walk perfectly upright with short bouncy steps. I humoured him and tried not to laugh, but after a while I noticed an improvement that made me feel more at ease in company. He made up a list of indelicate words and insisted that I stop using them. To improve my pronunciation he made me recite tongue-twisters with my mouth filled with pebbles from the river. For a long time I was scared I was going to swallow them and choke. I cursed my tormentor and wept to arouse his pity. I hurled the pebbles at his head, but in the end my lips and throat were so strengthened that I was able to make myself understood without raising my voice, even when Monsieur de Pompignac was standing on the opposite bank with the gurgling stream between us.

We also practised less tangible skills, such as enlarging the radius of projection of the personality and commanding attention in the middle of a busy market square by doing nothing more than controlling one's breathing and adopting a tranquil, regal pose. Don't ask me how it's possible, but I acquired this ability and have used it to my advantage ever since. Between all this, de Pompignac still found time to teach me simple dances like the bourrée and the farandole. We ate together so that I could get used to eating from a plate of my own instead of sharing the serving dish. He also insisted that I stop eating with my hands. I told him about my grandfather, who would scoop up some polenta with just three fingers, shape it into a little bowl on the palm of his hand, then fill it with meat and gravy and fold it in on itself. He ate like this at the most distinguished tables without spilling as much as a drop of sauce. He had practised all his life to achieve that level of dexterity. In our region this was the kind of thing that earned people's respect, and I had always been determined to strive for the same perfection and dignity. Monsieur de Pompignac, however, insisted that eating with a spoon and a fork was rated much more highly, even though anyone can master that in the course of a single meal. To raise my enthusiasm he made me a gift of a travelling set of silver cutlery, taking the opportunity to voice the hope that soon I might also learn to control my belching.

New infinite fields of knowledge opened up before me – page after page, book after book. It was dizzying. I was blind to everything else and leapt around in this freedom like a foal that has been put out in the meadow for the first time. I was too slow to notice my parents' growing concern and the way they were observing me from behind the fence of their simplicity. Coming home at the end of the day, I still told them everything I had seen and experienced. It was just that – instead of talking about familiar things from their own world, leaves that had started smouldering in the tobacco shed or an adder on the path – I now told stories about a nymph who changes into a laurel to save herself from being ravaged or a Corinthian queen who takes revenge on her husband by slaughtering their children. My parents took it all in and at first they even commented and gave advice ('Maybe that's better for the queen. Now she might find a gentle husband who can give her new children.') but after a while they just smiled and nodded without knowing what to say. My enthusiasm hurt them; I could see that, but I couldn't understand why. To spare my parents, I stopped talking about my new discoveries. This only depressed them more, convincing them that I thought them too stupid to understand – which had never occurred to me. My inability to see what they were going through was actually proof of *my* ignorance. When a more educated person interacts with someone less educated, it is the duty, and the privilege, of the former to adapt to the latter. The educated cannot fall back on the excuse that the others have by their very nature.

In late November I noticed their spirits picking up. They were gloating about something, that was obvious, but when I asked them about it, they wouldn't say a word. On the first Sunday of Advent I awoke to find my parents beaming next to my bed. My father was holding something behind his back, which he handed to me after a brief, rehearsed speech. What it came down to was that they were proud of me and wanted to support me as much as their limited capacities allowed, and that was why they were now giving me the first book I would own for myself. I removed the tissue paper and recognised it immediately. It was a copy of *Birth, Light and Promise of Christ the Saviour, Explained for the Holy Advent*, an essay by Fra Onofrio, our village priest. He had taken his simple thoughts on the subject – enough for a few rustic sermons – inflated them with borrowed terminology, random scientific terms and meaningless frills, and bound the result in calfskin so that he could flog it off to the parish dignitaries, who were too worried about the salvation of their souls to refuse. Less than a week before, he had palmed a copy off on Monsieur de Pompignac. Together we had laughed heartily about so much bombast and stupidity in one volume. Now I leafed through it again, under my parents' hopeful eyes. I was overcome by repugnance for the priest, who knew exactly how hard my father worked and how much he had denied himself and his family to save the price of this gilt-edged botch job. The fact that Fra Onofrio had not dissuaded my father from the purchase proved that Voltaire, whose work we had just begun reading, was right about the innate wickedness of the clergy. I turned the book over and over in my hands. I saw two equally painful options: telling the truth, taking the monstrosity back to our spiritual shepherd, cancelling the purchase and demanding the return of the money; or feigning gratitude and pretending to be so overcome that I didn't know how to respond. I chose the latter, resolving to pay back the money my parents had invested in me, with interest, once I was married to Giacomo and his career had begun. I hugged my mother and father. Afraid that I wouldn't be able to sustain the charade, I ran off, shouting that I had to show it to Monsieur de Pompignac immediately. In reality I was very careful to keep the book out of sight and did not dare to mention the incident to him.

For the first time I realised how far I had come in how short a period. Too far to ever find my way back home again.

Monsieur de Pompignac must have noticed something in my mood because he was unusually lenient that day. At dinner he chose the Fall as the subject of our daily discussion.

'Adam and Eve know it will cost them their innocence,

and still they want to eat from the Tree of Knowledge. How foolish would one need to be, Lucia, to renounce Paradise?'

'Our ancestors had no concept of Paradise until the moment it was denied them. In that sense it was wise to ignore God's prohibition. It taught them to value the beauty of the place they came from.'

'Do you think that this knowledge made them happier?'

'Surely you don't mean that it would be better to remain ignorant of the good, than to know that the good exists somewhere and . . .'

'. . . and realise you've squandered it. What do you think?'

'Absolutely not,' I exclaimed indignantly, as this was something he had just taught me, 'consciousness is our greatest good!'

'So a difficult life with knowledge would be preferable to a carefree existence that is not lived consciously.'

'Knowledge consoles,' I said. 'By analysing our grief about that lost paradise, our mind reduces it.'

'But wouldn't it be easier simply not to have any worries?'

'You make knowledge sound like an imperfection instead of an achievement.'

'Knowledge makes us aware of what we lack. It *is* an achievement but, like every form of wealth, it robs us of our carefreeness and innocence, just as it did Adam and Eve.' He paused here for a moment and then continued more gently, 'I have reason to believe that you too have now felt this sorrow.'

In a flash I saw my parents' hopeful faces as I leafed through the gift they had scrimped and saved to buy.

'I've had an inkling of the tears you warned me about when you started teaching me.'

'Gathering knowledge and acquiring skills are only the first steps. Anyone can do that. What follows is the real test, a test that defeats almost everyone: finding the courage to pick up one's baggage and walk away from the world, leaving other people further and further behind.'

I nodded.

'This realisation,' he said thoughtfully, 'is the diploma for my lessons.'

That evening we did not continue our discussion as pupil and teacher, but spoke openly as friends, with the exception that de Pompignac did not once allow me to deviate from French.

In a very short period my life at Pasiano had changed radically. I no longer visited the forests or fields that had once meant so much to me, instead I found my freedom in the manor house, which I was allowed to roam with so few restrictions that I almost forgot that I didn't belong there.

One day Count Antonio joined me in the library. He demonstrated his interest in my studies by pulling out a volume from his secret collection. It was the lavishly illustrated *Histoire de Dom Bougre, portier des Chartreux*. The old man came up behind me and put the book down on the table in front of me. Every time he turned a page he pressed his body up against mine. I told him in French that I didn't appreciate his attentions.

'Not yet, perhaps!' was his amused reply. He opened the book at a page that showed a courtesan obliging an officer with her tongue. 'You can learn to talk like a lady, but how do you think women like that afford the high life?' He laid his hand on the engraving and tickled the paper with his fat fingers, as if joining the illustrated characters in their play.

'Look, a trick like this brings in an easy three sequins,' he said seriously, 'remember that. Maybe even five, if it's done well.'

I stood up and hurried off to my lesson. Glancing back from the door, I saw the nobleman bent over his art collection. He seemed to have forgotten me already.

★

At the start of February, de Pompignac went off without telling me, interrupting our lessons for the first time. I spent the free days poring over the *Lettres persanes*, enjoying the experience of seeing all the things we take for granted through the eyes of an outsider. I could not possibly suspect that I would soon become one myself. Four days later Monsieur drove up to the house in a gig filled with festive packages, looking run-down but with a self-satisfied smile on his face. He kept his surprise to himself for three or four days, but after that he could no longer contain himself and told me the story.

He had travelled to Venice and back, not directly, but via Modena in order to waste as little of our instruction period as possible. This route allowed him to circumvent the nine-day quarantine that the Serenissima had imposed, officially for sanitary reasons but in reality to force the recalcitrant council of Friuli into submission.

'Be that as it may,' he laughed, 'the whole venture was for you. *Voilà!*' He handed me a pasteboard box with an enormous rosette, and beamed at me while I opened it. It contained a ball gown of dark-blue velvet. 'Beauty like yours needs no embellishment, but when people reach into a fruit bowl they can't help choosing a pear with a beautiful leaf.' It was the most gorgeous garment I had ever seen. I don't remember what exactly I thought – that I was supposed to adjust the dress, keep it for someone or starch and iron it – but although de Pompignac repeated that it was a gift for me, it was almost incomprehensible that he really wanted me to wear something so precious. Once it had sunk in, I pushed the dress away in fright, almost as if he had made a dishonourable proposition.

'I am nowhere near what you are trying to make of me,' I said, 'and I balk at the idea of presenting myself as such.'

He asked me to trust his judgement.

'If it's premature, we'll know soon enough,' he reassured

me. 'Count Antonio is giving a party for carnival. You will be the guest of honour. It's all been arranged. Unbeknownst to you, the old gentleman admires you and has shown a great interest in the progress you have been making. Don't say a word, all the dignitaries of the department have been invited, it would be out of the question to insult them by cancelling it at such short notice.' Then he pulled out the rest of my new wardrobe, piece by piece, as elated as if the gifts had been for him. Each new item delighted him as much as if he were seeing it for the first time, 'Shoes, ankle boots, aren't they gorgeous! Gloves, silk chemises – feel it, just feel it – a petticoat and a corset – all brand-new!'

When he saw that the prospect of a public examination depressed me, he laid it all aside to come and sit down next to me.

'There's nothing to worry about, *ma Galathée*! No one will know it's you.' As the last item, he pulled out one of the leather masks that people wore at that time. 'I shall introduce you as my niece . . .' He glowed with anticipation. '. . . *Je vous présente ma nièce, Galathée de Pompignac!*'

'You overestimate me.'

'We shall see,' he laughed and kissed me on both cheeks as if he really were my uncle.

We didn't see anything.

The next morning he didn't appear for my lesson at the usual time. In the night his throat had begun to swell. By the end of the day the dreaded fever had come, and the next morning, as expected, his mouth and tongue were covered with blisters. These were the signs of an aggressive smallpox pustule in his airways. The apothecary attributed the infection to Monsieur de Pompignac's foolish flouting of the Venetian quarantine and informed us that, given his age, he would only last two or three weeks at the most.

I wanted to keep my good friend company, but my

parents forbade it. The next day de Pompignac was transferred to an outhouse on the edge of the estate. My father took his possessions from his room, piled them up in a field and set fire to them. He wanted to throw his books onto the pile as well, but I stopped him. I told my father that the superstition that the disease attached itself to paper was backward and had been disproved by science. My parents looked at me with hurt expressions, but I had no choice. This was the first time I deployed my new-found authority, and I did it without thinking. It was only after I had gathered up the unburnt books and was walking away with them in my arms that I felt a quiet sorrow that these people who loved me deeply had deferred to my judgement so meekly.

After this they did not dare deny me access to my teacher a second time. I was the only one who entered his room without fear. The servants left his food and water on the threshold; I carried it in, sat down on his bed and read from the works that were so dear to him. I took it upon myself to nurse him. While doing so, I adhered meticulously to all the precautions, disinfecting both him and myself after each procedure. I wore a mask that had been drenched in alcohol and burnt all the leftover food and anything else he had touched. According to the latest insights, the patient could not be contagious in these circumstances. I tried to convince the others that there was nothing to fear, but it was no use. When his condition began deteriorating rapidly just a few days later, Fra Onofrio was only willing to administer the last rites through the window.

'What do you think, Lucia,' de Pompignac asked towards the end, in a tone that suggested that he was still strong enough to argue the case, 'who is better off, someone who dies unexpectedly or a condemned man who can count the days he has left?'

'They both lose the same,' I said cleverly, 'the day itself.'

My remark seemed to plunge him into such deep thought

that I blurted out a platitude to cheer him up, 'After all, if I went walking in the mountains today, I could be crushed by a falling boulder.'

'There is a very significant difference,' he said calmly, as if giving a lecture, 'and I am surprised that you don't see it. Imagine that you and I are standing under that boulder. You see it slipping and run away, then skip off home afterwards. I see it too. It is hanging over my head. It wobbles. I see it tilting. I call out to you, "It's going to fall!" It slides free. I see it coming towards me. And all this time I am there under it, waiting for the blow with my foot caught in a wolf trap.'

I was ashamed of myself. In my haste to comfort the dying man, I had resorted to the kind of cliché people always use when trying to disguise their impotence.

'It's nothing to brood about,' de Pompignac assured me. 'Your emotions were too strong for your intellect. That proves that all the knowledge I have inundated you with has not stifled your heart. Heart and mind, the combination at the apex of human achievement. I couldn't have asked for a more beautiful parting gift.'

I then tried to feed him the honeyed pap that was the last thing he could swallow. Using my silver spoon, I ate some too, and we acted as if this were just one of the many dinners we had eaten together.

He lay back and spoke his last words.

'*Mes félicitations*, Lucia, at last you've eaten a whole meal without a single belch!'

The Countess of Montereale showed her gratitude for Monsieur de Pompignac's contribution to her daughter's happiness by returning to Pasiano for his funeral. As she was held up en route, my teacher's burial was delayed beyond the legal limit. Finally, in the dead of night, my patroness arrived. The next morning, to surprise her while also honouring him, I put on the dress he had given me. I combed my hair and put it up according to the latest fashion. Despite the sadness of the occasion, I swirled around a few times as if at a ball and practised the curtsy I would use to greet the countess.

When I went into her room, the old lady was still in bed. At first she didn't understand who I was. Even after I had told her my name, she was still confused. It wasn't until I said something in my old dialect and leapt onto her bed like before, that she was prepared to believe that I really was her Lucia. I opened the shutters so that she could see me properly and cuddled up next to her. For a few moments she was overcome with joy as she struggled to take in the full extent of my metamorphosis.

Then her gaze went to my face.

In an instant all the happiness drained from her expression. She recoiled in shock and started screaming. To calm her, I took her hand, but that only made things worse. Like a cornered animal, she crept backward out of the bed and pressed herself up against the wall in an attempt to get as far away from me as possible. She grabbed a handkerchief, poured eau de cologne over it, and held it up to her mouth, gesturing furiously for me to keep my distance. I still had no idea why the surprise I had looked forward to so much had misfired so badly.

The disappointment was too much for me.

I doubled over and fell to the floor, racked by a sorrow that was beyond my comprehension. Before fleeing the room, the countess looked at me one last time. Tears were running down her face; she was as tormented by the shock as I was.

'Dear child, poor child,' she sobbed, trembling, 'my darling girl, who will ever give you love now?'

2

Too much of our knowledge of ourselves is derived from the gaze of others. We are more willing to rely on how we are seen than on how we see ourselves.

My mother rushed into the room. I was still sobbing on the floor. She had been alerted by the countess and squatted before me. She took my head in her hands and studied a lump on my cheek. Her eyes were wild. In them I saw both pity and fear. Only then did I realise which calamity had come upon me.

She let go of me, got up off the floor and stood there like a statue, towering above me with her arms stretched out as if they were suddenly filthy.

This time none of my cries could mollify my parents. Volume by volume, I saw the library Monsieur de Pompignac had left me consumed by fire. Then my father fed the flames with the ball gown. Scraps of blue fabric spiralled up on the smoke. Finally, when almost everything had been reduced to ash, they found the mask Monsieur had bought for me in Venice and threw it on the coals. The smouldering leather gave off a nauseating stench. Dirty yellow smoke rose up through the eyes while the cheeks and nose blistered and shrivelled. All of Monsieur's gifts went up in flames, together with his plans for my future. I was glad he hadn't lived to see it. Then I thought of my father and mother, who would have to watch my downfall from close by. Given the circumstances, they were coping well. I was moved to that same building on the edge of the estate – after they had smoked the room with juniper. I lay down on the bed I had spent the last few days sitting beside. Here I finally calmed down. I closed my eyes and saw Giacomo.

In my thoughts, he was sitting beside me, pressing his hands against my cheeks and hushing me, constantly whispering that I had nothing to be afraid of because love would conquer all. I knew perfectly well that this was a fantasy, but it still made me feel a little less miserable. I calculated how much time would have to pass before my fiancé really could hold me tight. My beloved had promised to return to Pasiano at Easter for our engagement. The disease had felled me several days before carnival. My fate, according to my calculations, would be decided in less than seven weeks.

At that stage I took two possibilities into account: death or recovery. I could imagine them both. Easily. My imagination is very vivid. Every horror or reprieve, possible or impossible, appears to me in such detail that when it finally comes about I feel as though I recognise it. This weakness, which so often afflicts sensitive natures, is also a strength. Although it can redouble the mind's suffering or cause unnecessary anguish, it is also a way of hardening oneself and preparing for the worst.

For two days there was no change. In the night that followed, the pain struck. I winced as if being stabbed with daggers. New lesions appeared on my upper arms. The disease was taking its external form. According to the apothecary, this, combined with my youth, increased my chance of survival. A third possibility – besides dying or simply recovering – now occurred to me.

The thought terrified me.

I asked to be tied up. My parents didn't have the heart to do it. I begged them, pleading and in tears, but when they still hesitated, I cursed and raged as if they were obstinate servants, and ordered them to do it for love's sake. I lay on my back with my legs spread. My father used a rope to lash my feet to the bars at the foot of the bed. My mother tied my wrists with a silk cord, which they passed under the bed and tightened with a cleat. I told them not to release me under any circumstances, no matter how much I begged, until I was fully recovered or – if God ordained it so – had died.

In this position I waited.

Every hour brought new abscesses, while the old ones only seemed to swell.

After three days the pain suddenly subsided. For the first time I slept all night, despite the discomfort and the stiffness of my muscles.

An itch woke me. It tickled up the inside of my thighs. It didn't worry me, and in my dreamy, drowsy state, I experienced it as a most pleasurable sensation. Then the itch spread outwards: first down my legs to the soles of my feet and in between my toes. I bent them. I spread them. I tugged at the ropes. They chafed but gave no relief. Then that same prickling began between my shoulder blades. I rubbed myself on the sheet as best I could, to no effect. The fire was now smouldering at the base of my throat and flickering between my breasts. From there it crept up to my nipples, where my skin was already stretched to the limit by the accumulated fluids; there wasn't an inch of undamaged skin visible anywhere on my whole trunk. I arched my back and jerked my shoulders, but gained no respite. Now the prickling flared up and began licking at my arms, my hands and my fingers. I was scared that if I couldn't find some way of scratching myself I would surely lose my mind.

Then I felt the tingling behind my eyelids. It surprised me. By this time so much of the rest of my body was ablaze that I was convinced my torment could not possibly grow worse. Anyone who hasn't been through something similar might find it hard to believe, but at that moment I really seemed to have forgotten that my face, the very reason I had ordered my parents to bind me, had until then been spared. Slowly the itch spread up over it as well.

I realised that the moment had arrived, my worst fears were about to come true.

I panicked, making the fire flare up even higher and sweep over my body in new bursts. Forehead, lips, ears, chin and cheeks, the worms of torment seemed to be squirming everywhere, even to the ends of my hair. They crept down my neck and wriggled out over all four of my limbs.

I screamed. My mother came running. I now used the same tone in which I had implored her to tie me up and remain deaf to my entreaties to beg her to release me. The poor woman covered her ears with her hands and refused to obey. I responded by forcing myself to calm down and take a cleverer approach. I talked about something else for a moment, then slipped in a casual remark that I had been mistaken at the outset of my disease, that it wasn't necessary for me to be tied up, and that at this stage it only worsened my condition. If she loved me and cared about me, I said, she really should release me now. This set her to doubting. I could see that. In my imagination I was already pulling myself free and sighing with relief as I scratched my wounds open with all ten fingernails. But I controlled myself and remained silent to increase the effect. I smiled reassuringly to encourage my mother and speed her decision. She remained silent. She paced through the room a number of times, hesitated and then refused after all. I turned into a demon. I vomited such a torrent of cruel filth out over her that she fled the room in tears without acceding to any of my demands.

I was on fire without any hope of its ever being extinguished.

Delivered up to this torture and beset by fevers, I took the only escape I could see. The impulse was natural and beyond all doubt, like the urge to run out of a burning house. I detached myself from my body and abandoned it. It was as if I was fleeing to take shelter in my soul, where I now hid, trembling in a corner.

At first I only saw delirious fantasies. They raged like a storm, but I still preferred them to reality. Slowly I felt as though I could pick out patterns in the midst of the whirlwind. Ideas detached themselves, and I tried to seize onto them and organise them. After a while I was able to separate them out, one from the other. I recognised childhood memories, my old expectations of my future, the fear of having to surrender them, my desire for Giacomo, my grandfather's hands and smile, the overseer's dogs, and the good lessons Monsieur de Pompignac had taught me. I was able to classify them more and more clearly, ordering them according to the philosophers he and I had considered together, who now came to my aid for the first time.

By analysing each new nightmare in this way – dissecting them to isolate and identify their constituent elements – I learnt to control them. This did not come without a struggle, and there were regular outbursts of thoughts that threatened to overwhelm me, but each time my mind succeeded where my emotions had failed, and I forced them back into place.

I created order from chaos and, almost without noticing, gradually compiled the encyclopaedia of my own life. On a much smaller scale but essentially the same as Chambers'

Cyclopaedia or the project that Diderot has begun, mine allowed me first to understand and ultimately to control myself and the situation. It worked. The storm subsided. I had snared it with my reason, just as sailors claim to catch the winds in a sailor's knot.

This was the turning point. If it could help me through a trial like this, I told myself, the power of reason could save me in any situation. This seemed to give meaning to my illness, as if everything was subordinate to this realisation. I resolved that, if I survived, I would let reason guide me for the rest of my life. After reaching this decision, I dared to abandon my fortress in the clouds and return to the ruins of my body.

The fever subsided.

The itch died down.

I regained consciousness and saw my parents at my bedside with Fra Onofrio's frightened face in the window behind them. From this safe distance, the priest was busily administering the last rites. I thanked him and told him that I would not be needing his services.

My words had an astonishing effect. My father began to cry – something I had never seen before – my mother fell to her knees before me and Onofrio turned as white as a ghost and ducked down under the window sill. Apparently I had been dead to the world for three weeks, after which they had surrendered all hope and released me from my restraints. Just when they were expecting me to breathe my last, I had spoken in a loud, clear voice.

From the garden Onofrio called out that my recovery was an act of God, a special divine intervention in honour of Palm Sunday, and an indisputable miracle the like of which he had not seen before in all his years as a priest. I answered that he was a fool and his God nothing more than an invention to explain the incomprehensible to ninnies, whereupon he fled and my mother crossed herself three times.

Either way, I was cured and it was Palm Sunday! That gave me a full week to build up my strength before Giacomo arrived. I immediately asked for broth and fruit and red meat. My appetite was back and I feasted on all the things the others were denying themselves because of Lent. I drank as much as I could and gargled with malmsey to banish the evil taste from my mouth. This initial period of convalescence was so exhausting that I fell into a deep sleep after every meal, but awoke every time feeling invigorated and stronger.

On the morning of the third day I was ready. I wanted to try to walk around a little and wash myself. My parents brought me facecloths and a jug of water, clean underwear and a starched chemise, a hairbrush, soap and lavender water. Finally, I asked for a mirror.

My father and mother exchanged a glance.

I saw the look in their eyes and knew everything.

My precautions had saved my body from the worst. Tied up throughout my frenzy, I had been unable to scratch and wound myself with my nails. Of the hundreds of pocks that had covered me from my throat to my toes, only a few had ulcerated. Here and there, I still had the scabs. My body would be left with small permanent marks in those places, but it was nothing disfigured.

That couldn't be said of my face.

My parents were reluctant to bring me a mirror so soon. To spare them unnecessary sorrow, I pretended that I was happy to wait. The moment they left, I pulled out my grandfather's pendant. It was small, but big enough. I saw myself through *Santa Lucia*'s eyes.

The ropes that held me down had been unable to prevent me from thrashing around with my head. Furiously I had beaten my cheeks against the mattress, trying to somehow tear open my eyelids, which were clagged up with pus. Later my mother told me that they had tried to hold my head, which had swelled up by a third, and reduce the burning with wet rags. For a long time she sat behind me, trying to protect my face by keeping my head clamped between her knees and hands. To no avail. The itch was too intense, the torment too great. Nothing could restrain me. I gave in to the dictates of the nature of my disease and rubbed myself wherever I could – cheeks, forehead, ears, mouth and nose – turning even the softest pillow and the finest sheet into instruments of mutilation.

After all these years, I still find it difficult to describe the ruin I saw in that mirror. Suffice to say that I didn't recognise myself. Taut red skin was growing over what must have been one big open wound. In time this new skin would heal, albeit unevenly, with deep craters and thick lumps. The left side of my face, however, was devastated for ever by distorted, contracting scars.

I sat and stared into the pendant. Hypnotised by my own reflection, I was no longer able to look through the glass and see that behind it, as always, even through this apparition, my grandfather's decorative artistry was glittering and shining in the sunlight.

Giacomo arrived earlier than expected, on Good Friday. In the intervening days I had considered all the steps I could possibly take, but couldn't bring myself to make a final decision.

I saw my love through the chinks of my closed shutters. He strode across the courtyard in his best clothes, hurrying, elated, excited to be back and anxious to see me again.

I was fifteen. Eighty years would not have been long enough to amass enough experience for the decision I had to make. I had never left my place of birth. The rest of the world was something I knew only from books. Beyond

Pasiano, the only life I could imagine was the life people led in Venice, but *that* I could picture vividly and all too clearly. Thanks to the countess, I was thoroughly convinced of the mercilessness of the better circles in Venice, where looks were everything. My 'aunt' had hoped to strengthen me for the struggle that would await someone of my humble origins there, but now that my illness had changed everything, it was her words, more than anything, that cut off the path to my future happiness.

After all, I could never be accepted in that city now that I was disfigured. I would be a pariah. And if Giacomo married me, he would share my fate.

As this realisation sank in, I drifted into a peculiar calm. Just days before, during my fever, I had clung to reason when all else failed me. Now I decided to rely on my intellect once again. I *was* aware of my emotions, dear God, how I was aware of them! My heart pounded, my soul was screaming. And all the while I followed his steps across the courtyard from my gloomy vantage point behind the shutters.

Giacomo had changed from a boy to a man and was much more handsome than I remembered him. If I hadn't fought against the urge with all my might, I would have run to him and thrown myself at his feet. I would have told him the whole story and begged him to take me as I was.

I suppressed it all. In my pillow I smothered several loud screams that seemed to come straight from my soul. Everything was raw inside. My emotions were on their knees and ready to surrender to my reason.

After this first shock, the cool deliberation came as a comfort, just as the shock of the cold bath that was prepared for me after my illness made all the scars on my body contract and helped my skin to relax.

This was my dilemma: Giacomo was the personification of my happiness. If he chose to accept me despite my disfigurement, we could marry. I would have my love by my side for the rest of my life. This, however, would require him to surrender his ambitions. Our marriage would preclude any chance of a career. This would make him unhappy, and it would be a torment for me to see him suffer. His unhappiness would become mine as well. Following my heart now would be the ruin of us both.

But if I acted counter to my emotions by leaving him free, I would allow him to pursue and realise his dreams. Although I would be unhappy, I could console myself by knowing that he would find happiness. He might be sad about me for a while, but if I played it so that he believed that I had betrayed him, his sadness would be brief. Then he would grow angry, curse me and, in the end, forget me.

That was my reasoning.

The first course of action produced two unhappy people; the second, only one.

The choice seemed simple.

I acted like a machine, ignoring my emotions and disowning them loudly three times.

I took the steps I had to take with the determination I had once seen in a peasant from Portobuffolè called Zoldo, who had been bitten by an adder before my eyes. Shocked, I tried to reassure him by talking in a soothing voice, but he neither saw nor heard me. His veins swelled and turned black. Calm as a walking corpse, he did what he had to do. He took a saw, cut off his leg below the knee and cauterised the stump to stop the bleeding – all without a moment's hesitation.

With that same assuredness and those same paralysed emotions, I gave my mother the task of telling Giacomo that I had left Pasiano. Appalled at the idea of lying to the man whose love for me equalled her own, she refused to tell him that I was no longer there.

Then I told her that today's lie would be true enough

tomorrow. Giacomo would be sure to come back. It was impossible for me to stay.

She was so shattered that she offered no further resistance. I told her that if my fiancé asked about my feelings for him, she should tell him that was all in the past; I had run off with the courier L'Aigle without so much as a message as to where we were going. There was absolutely no sense in his keeping up any hopes or waiting for me.

By the time she entered the garden room, which had once again been made ready for Giacomo, my mother's face was so tear-stained that he had no choice but to believe her. It took him a full hour to recover after hearing the news. Then he was given a pastry to regain his strength, and some fruit and bread for the journey home.

In the meantime I summoned reason to my aid, requested an audience with Count Antonio and told him that I had come to earn the five sequins, if his offer still stood. His astonishment was short-lived. The old man studied the damage to my appearance through his lashes. For a moment he considered bargaining me down because of it, but decided not to. He opened a drawer and laid the money on the table. Then leant back on his chair, unbuttoned his trousers and told me to undress slowly before him.

Don't think I found it so terribly disgusting. It was something that had to happen, that's all. I am not one of those women who have an innate abhorrence of physicality and can only bring themselves to it when moved by a deep sense of love. On the contrary, I am carnal by nature. I knew at an early age that it would suit me.

At some stage in the proceedings I realised that the pragmatism of this transaction was also consistent with the new image I needed to form of myself. There were clear borders. That made me feel better. Within these limits I felt sure of myself. More than that, it was important for me to see that someone could still desire me, despite my ugliness; I had not been completely ruined as a woman.

I would have given anything to discover this pleasure for the first time with Giacomo, but I resigned myself to the reality. The old man mounted me and had his way. He was overjoyed to discover that I was still a virgin and spent an eternity studying this phenomenon at close-hand, using his fat fingers to spread me as wide as possible. When he finally entered me, he clapped his hands like a child.

Even the coarsest of men are no longer terrifying once they are in bed. They can be hard and thoughtless, but their elation leaves no room for calculation. When they have full command of their faculties they can inflict pain deliberately, but if they hurt you in bed, it is only out of awkwardness. They become as easy to please as children, and once pleased they are just as grateful.

I pleasured the Count of Montereale and derived a certain satisfaction in doing so. I am not proud of it, but it is a fact. Later, too, I sometimes let men who disgusted me have their way with me. I pleasured these fellows – moronic, misshapen or decrepit – with no other object than the hope that one day someone might do the same for me when I needed it: once again giving me the feeling that I was beautiful and desirable.

As far as Count Antonio's sweating body was concerned, my mind came to my aid again. I discovered that I could look at that quivering flesh and flushed face, and even smile at it, without actually seeing it. It didn't come back to me in my nightmares either.

Imagination is the best sanctuary.

There, and only there, I was together with Giacomo, that night and many others.

3

It was still dark when I left the house. I didn't say goodbye to my parents, scared as I was that their sorrow would hold me captive. Their love had brought me this far. Now it was up to me to go further. Together with de Pompignac I had taken the first step. For the second, I had his words to guide me: it was time for me to pick up my baggage and walk away from the world. From the kitchen I took one of the wicker baskets hunters use to carry pheasants. Their wide straps let you carry quite a weight on your shoulders. Not that I had much to carry. My clothes took up almost no space at all. When no one was looking, I slipped into the count's library and picked out several books that I had promised Monsieur de Pompignac to read one day. On impulse, I also pulled the *Histoire de Dom Bougre, portier des Chartreux* out of its secret hiding place. Although I had no claim to this valuable work, I did not hesitate for a moment. My conscience told me that I had earned it. Perhaps I also hoped that my thieving might make the count think twice before forcing another young girl to look at his pornography. Either way, I knew that these pictures were a great rarity and that I could sell them to raise money I might very well need.

Weighed down like this, I took the road to Vilotta, reaching the village at first light. The peasants were already heading out to their land. As most of them knew me, I hid in a ditch on the side of the road to avoid being recognised. Slowly I began to sense the gravity of the adventure that awaited me. I had only just left the farmlands of Pasiano and already my legs felt like lead. The straps of the basket were cutting into my back. For a moment I was afraid that the sleep that had evaded me in the previous night might overcome me now, but I resisted. An unknown strength was growing inside me and keeping me alert. Despite lacking both plan and purpose, I felt neither fear nor regret. On the contrary, I was filled with a strange joy. It seemed almost improper. I was leaving everything I knew behind me. I had lost everything I loved. Reckless but determined, I was giving up my life for ever, just as yesterday I had given up Giacomo. I was almost ashamed at feeling so excited despite my sorrow, and wondered how it was possible. This exuberance stayed with me for weeks and spurred me on at crucial moments. I headed south – mainly because the Alps seemed like an unnecessary complication – reaching Rovigo first and then Ferrara. From there, after spending a long time wandering over the plain, I came to Bologna. All this time, my heart was overflowing. Life had revealed its true face and I was burning with excitement. We stood opposite each other like two rivals on the morning of a duel, menacing but well matched.

I liked Bologna. There were more people there than I had ever seen in one place before. That made it easier for me to blend in. If someone started pointing, I slipped away between the customers at the market, and when children started following me, I disappeared down one of the crowded lanes. But life was harder than in the country.

People had no qualms about openly commenting on my appearance. It hurt, but in the end remarks made in the open are less damaging than the same remarks made behind your back. Finding work in a city wasn't easy either. When there are plenty of beautiful girls available, nobody chooses an ugly one. I was forced to show other qualities. By trying harder than the rest, asking for less money and putting up with more, I managed to find job after job. In the process I turned a blind eye to humiliation and pawing. I learnt to accept things that other women refused to tolerate, a lesson that later proved very valuable. Still, my jobs never lasted long. Once, when I was serving in an eating-house, someone shouted that my poxy mug was spoiling his appetite, but the signs were usually more subtle. The trade fell off in shops when I was behind the counter; after I started taking the minutes for a lawyer, a number of clients stopped coming; and the daughters of the family I briefly cleaned for were scared to come near me. Rather than wait for my employers to broach the subject, I usually resigned of my own accord and started searching for a new position. Looking back on it now, it's hard to believe that I didn't lose heart completely, but somehow I persevered. When you are as young as I was then, even the most dismal failure can help you to find your way forward.

After several months, I found employers who put results above appearances and were willing to provide me with food and lodging in exchange for work. They were a married couple, the Morandi Manzolinis. He was attached to the Accademia delle Scienze, where he taught anatomy. As he couldn't bear the sight of blood, his wife, Anna, did the dissections for him. She produced exact wax models of the skulls she opened and the organs she removed, and *these* her husband used for his lectures. She also did her own research. In the daytime I cooked and kept house – something she had no talent for – and at night I was free to study. The Morandi

Manzolinis had no objection to my reading and after a while they even granted me access to their library. When they had guests, I was allowed to engage help. They gave me a large sum of money to spend as I saw fit on the preparations for the feast. Penniless as I was, I could easily have cheated them.

'How can someone ever prove themselves worthy of your trust, if you don't give it to them first?' the signora explained when she noticed my surprise at so much unworldliness. 'When you give someone responsibility, they take it.' She then launched into a discourse on the way in which women had, for a long time, forgotten how to think for themselves because their husbands made all the decisions, and assured me that the new scientific discoveries would finally put an end to this by challenging male and female intellects to an equal degree. I took this to heart and never brought domestic matters to her attention again.

She addressed her visitors the same way. Most of them were like-minded and they all came from the best families. They reinforced each other in the belief that women were selling themselves short by trusting to their emotions and would never know true freedom until the day that the intellect triumphed over intuition for ever. They chattered away about this subject with a passion that inadvertently proved their argument. I never participated in their discussions, even though they repeatedly asked my opinion. When I refused outright, they still insisted. I thought it improper of them to embarrass a servant in this way, but they brushed my objections aside. They preached that the days of masters and servants were numbered and claimed that the world would soon be divided instead into the educated and the ignorant, a final inequality that anyone could erase simply by studying.

During these debates, I preferred to hide in the library. But their blind optimism was still infectious. Even when I disagreed with them, I enjoyed the way the atmosphere was charged with expectation. It strengthened my hope that in this climate even my future might one day take a turn for the better.

This optimism amongst the women of the city was fed by Prospero Lambertini, the former archbishop of Bologna and a cousin of Signora Manzolini, who in those years sat upon the papal throne as Benedict XIV. He provided lavish support for the university on the condition that it employed female scientists and recognised 'female knowledge and learning'. The Holy Father had gone so far as to promise chairs to several of them, including my mistress, Anna Morandi Manzolini, and her bosom friend, Laura Bassi. According to the signora, this proved that the belief in reason had supplanted the belief in the spirit for ever, even in Rome. Meanwhile a papal commission, together with a delegation of learned women, strove for official recognition by civil and academic authorities of 'female intelligence and intellectual capacities'. One day I was present at the drafting of a declaration to this effect that would be submitted to all academic institutes for ratification. *Femmes savantes* had come from all over Europe to the Morandi Manzolini residence for this occasion; I served them sardines.

It was hard work. In my months of service there I had never seen this many guests at one time. I was nervous, but thought of my mother, who at Pasiano had sometimes been responsible for ten times as many people. For me, however, it was something new. They had confused my knowledge with maturity and burdened me with tasks that were almost beyond me. Despite employing twelve people for the whole week, I scarcely had a moment to myself. For the first time, I had to give orders and trust that they would be carried out. I was surprised to discover that this required courage and self-assurance, qualities I was severely lacking at that time. The comments strangers had made about me in the streets had quickly eroded the confidence my loving parents had instilled in me. And the remnant that survived their assault was destroyed by a handsome student who spent several days courting me because of a dare. He finally told me so in front of the friends whose idea it had been, much to the hilarity of all present. Either way, by this time I rated the opinions of others much higher than my own. The responsibility Signora Morandi entrusted me with was my salvation. I grabbed the hand she held out to me and did my utmost to avoid disappointing her. At first I played the superiority I wanted to exercise over my twelve subordinates the way an actor plays a king, with a booming voice and borrowed gestures, as if I could shout down my ugliness, but gradually I noticed that they listened much better when I spoke to them as myself, being honest and open and occasionally letting them catch a glimpse of my doubts. I realised that by daring to ignore my looks, I could win people over with my character. The more I regained my respect for myself, the more I won theirs.

I had been instructed to treat all the guests as equals, regardless of rank or title. As the signora explained, 'They are all as wise as each other, and knowledge is the new aristocracy!' These women had names like Zenobia and Uranie, Alkmene, Celymene, Cleanthe and Anamandra, and I was overwhelmed by the unfamiliar sounds. During their debates, they called them out one after the other. I loved to listen while serving the coffee, just as I once delighted in the names of the fairies and witches in my father's bedtime stories. I saw them as queens of the intellect and tried to imagine the worlds they ruled over.

Their days were long. They spent the mornings lecturing each other on the disciplines in which they excelled, and dedicated their evenings to a less formal analysis of their loves and lives. In between they ate together. I stood next to the sideboard, behind a screen with a small window in it. From this discreet vantage point, I was able to make sure that the guests were being served correctly and that their glasses were being filled fast enough. I could also hear what they had to say; some spoke Latin, but most of them understood each other better in French. Every day they discussed new discoveries, regularly setting up flasks, alembics and retorts to carry out experiments. Hungry for knowledge as I was, I tried to understand as much as I could, but often it went over my head. I wasn't in any position to ask for an explanation, and my thoughts wandered. At times like that I would study the guests: their expressions and the way they reacted to things.

Only one of them spotted me in my hiding place. One day she caught my eye and held it with a look that was compelling, yet friendly. She was a French countess who stood out a little in the group. Although she was as well dressed as the others, as beautiful and as eloquent, they still seemed to exclude her from full membership of their coterie. When answering questions she was invariably good-natured, but she never raised a topic of conversation. She wore her bright-red hair up in a wide crown that required her to hold her neck straight and her head back a little, elegant and arrogant at once. I had heard her name a few times, but in that instant I was so shocked by the look in her eyes that I couldn't think of it. She was staring at me with a restlessness and a yearning I couldn't understand. For a moment I thought she had been crying. Her eyes were wet. I could see them gleaming. But her face conveyed the opposite. Her smile was determined and she carried herself with the pride of someone who is used to victory. I had every right to stand there watching over things, but still felt as if she had caught me out doing something wrong. I surveyed the table for a moment longer as if we had not exchanged glances at all, then waved for one of the servants to take my place so that I could beat a retreat and withdraw between my signora's books. I stayed hidden away in the library until the guests had gone to bed and the tables were cleared – indeed much longer. Not reading, but just sitting there between the medical, surgical, philosophical and astrological treatises, surrounded by Manzolini's scientific instruments and her wax models of body parts, arranged according to function. On the high shelves around me, all plant and animal species were described and illustrated, along with all known minerals and elements and their effects, applications and origins. Even the earth itself – with its continents and oceans, its towns and cities and the roads that led to them – was documented in some thirty atlases.

The profound peace I feel in libraries goes beyond silence. The paper doesn't just muffle sound, it also stills the roar of my thoughts. The overwhelming amount of knowledge in the bookcases consoles me. It is so much more than could ever fit into my brain. This calms my restless thoughts and reminds me that there is no necessity for me to know and understand everything. So much of it has been written down, and I have it all at my fingertips. It's no longer my responsibility. The world has been classified. Even though I will never be able to absorb more than a fraction of all these facts, they are there, they have been recorded. If I ever need them, I can look them up. A reality that is monitored and verifiable is so much easier to let go. Maybe that's the purpose of all these writers: by recording the outside world they liberate me and let me dedicate myself to my inner life.

In my mind, I began to map out my feelings and tried to trace the route I had followed. A year had passed since I had left Pasiano. In that time I had been forced to travel through the most remote regions of my emotional world, places where the climate fluctuated wildly. Sometimes I had to wade through poisoned lakes where all life was paralysed. I had crossed the most desolate landscapes with my eyes fixed straight ahead, like a skittish, blinkered horse being led through hostile territory. Only by keeping my eyes pinned on the road ahead was I able to cross the peaks and climb up out of the valleys without taking fright or being injured by the bombs landing left and right. This was how I managed to come through the whole voyage without losing my mind or abandoning all hope – often I was simply unaware of the precipice I was skirting. That was why I hadn't shed a tear since leaving. Now, for the first time, I could permit myself to pause and take in the view. The path seemed to have levelled off. What had been strange now seemed familiar. I thought I had distanced myself enough from my sorrow and finally dared to stop and take my bearings.

At some stage, while wandering through my emotions in this way, I must have fallen asleep. When I awoke I was looking into the eyes of the French countess. She was bending over me with one leg up on the seat of my couch, as if about to mount a horse.

'I am studying your face,' she said. 'What was it, smallpox?'

She towered over me. I was trapped and tried to sink back into the cushions. Her face looked pale under the hair that swelled and bulged above it, big and fiery like the setting sun. She stayed leaning over me, moving from left to right, then back again to assess the damage.

'It hurts now, but you'll be glad of it later. Beauty is a dungeon in which we languish. You've escaped it. At this stage, that insight does not help you at all. Later you will discover it yourself. I only ask that, when you do, you think back on the woman who told you about it for the first time.' With this, her curiosity seemed satisfied. She dismounted and turned away, as if she had lost all interest in me. For a while she walked along the walls studying the books. Now and then she picked one out and leafed through it. Finally, she ascended the wooden ladder, took a folio volume out from one of the top shelves, opened it and sat down to read, crossing her legs and hitching up her skirts like a peasant girl in a hayloft. This was so improper that I thought she must have forgotten that I was there. To avoid embarrassing her, I quietly picked a book up off the table and crept away.

'You read?' she asked.

'When I find the time.'

'There you have it. You're a servant, so I immediately assumed you couldn't read.' She jumped down from the ladder. 'That's how easily we make the mistake of judging others by their appearance.'

'Then beauty would seem to me to be even more of an advantage.'

'If someone sees something beautiful, he thinks it's finished. That satisfies him. He looks no further. He doesn't set to work. He doesn't dare to cut into it, and so we never discover what was lying beneath the surface. None of its hidden riches are revealed. That is why it pays not to carry your treasures on the outside. If rough diamonds were less ugly, it would never have occurred to anyone to cut the stone.'

'Very kind of you to say so,' I said indignantly. 'For someone who is so unplagued by it, you have a most profound understanding of ugliness.' I tried to leave but she blocked my path. She took the book from my hands, read the spine and seemed impressed that it was in French.

'Descartes, no less!' She stepped back to study me from head to toe, then looked around as if to make sure that no one was playing a joke on her. Meanwhile she smiled at me with the tip of her tongue sticking out between her teeth. 'Tell me now, seriously, where did Signora Morandi dig *you* up?' She took my hand and shook it, as if we were two men. 'I'm Zélide. And you?'

I was hurt. She was so open about my imperfection that I felt an urge to be secretive with her. The last thing I wanted was to tell her my real name. Girls called Lucia were as scarce in that area as flies around a horse's tail. I wanted to stop the countess from taking my humble origins as the basis for another one of her aristocratic little theories.

'My name is Galathée,' I replied, trying to outdo her. Her mouth dropped open, but I insisted.

'Galathée de Pompignac.'

She immediately burst out laughing. I was furious. I pulled my hand back and tried to leave, but she refused to let me go. Instead she grabbed me by the wrists and kissed both my hands, ignoring my discomfort.

'Well, Galathée de Pompignac, I needn't worry myself on your account, that's clear enough. You've already started to cut your own diamond. You're an absolute gem!' Then she kissed me again. On the cheek. The wrong one.

The next morning, when I was serving breakfast, Zélide caught my eye and winked as if we were friends. I suspected her of trying to impress the others by showing the ease with which she associated with her inferiors, and ignored her completely. My indifference seemed to upset her. She stood up and hurried out into the garden without touching her breakfast.

At ten o'clock, I brought cake and fruit in to the ladies and assumed my post behind the screen so that I could listen to their discussion, as I did every morning. They took turns to speak on the subject of the day: deriving energy from water. Most of them had a clear opinion, but Zélide remained aloof, and when I hurried off to get to the market on the Piazza Malpighi before noon, she defied etiquette by jumping up and following me into the kitchen. When I picked up a basket, she picked up another and, despite the impropriety, insisted on carrying it herself. At the stalls she squeezed the fruit, weighed the meat in her hand and discussed herbs like an expert. Meanwhile she told me that her father had been a teacher in a provincial town. She acted as if her origins were as humble as my own. I chose not to disabuse her. She was an only child and her father had taught her everything he knew, but for her that wasn't enough.

'I just happen to be shamelessly inquisitive,' she admitted, 'about everything and everyone. Don't you agree that, more than anything else, science is rampant indiscretion? A morbid urge to find out everything, even things you were never meant to know, things that can only disturb your peace of mind? When you investigate the qualities and principles of the elements, people consider it a virtue, but if you subjected *them* to a similar analysis, they would chase you off their land.'

Zélide had acquired her title by marrying the octogenarian Count of Montmorency. By burying him, she acquired the means to bring teachers from all over Europe to her home in Vincennes. Over the years, she had summoned more and more people from further and further afield because the thirst for knowledge only grows the more you try to quench it.

'I have noticed,' she remarked, after we got to know each other a little, 'the interest with which you follow our scientific discussions in the Morandi residence. But you never participate.'

'How could I? I scarcely understand most of the things you say.'

'Then you should ask us to clarify them.'

'I am in too much awe of all that knowledge to speak up.'

'Ah, if some of us could follow that example! Speaking about something one does not understand is foolish, asking about it is wise. What is science, if not admitting one's ignorance? After all, you can only learn something you don't know.'

'And since I know much less than you,' I laughed, 'that makes me the greater scholar of the two of us.'

'I will be leaving Bologna tomorrow morning,' Zélide said as we returned home with full baskets. 'I am travelling on to

Naples. There are some new excavations there. At the foot of Mount Vesuvius a number of ancient Roman villas have been exposed, perfectly intact. This is the heart of our epoch. At last, the ash that smothers us is being blown away. Everything is coming to the surface. A light will shine on things that are still shrouded in gloom. Nothing will be left unexplained. This is the challenge of the century. The discoverers form the vanguard. Our place is beside them. I shall be there and you ... I would like to ask you to accompany me.'

'Why?'

'As my secretary.' She blushed and searched for the right words. Among all those learned, wealthy women she had been able to maintain her authority, and it tickled me that I of all people had now thrown her off-balance.

'If you want to take me under your wing out of charity . . .' I couldn't understand the source of her affection for me and remained cautious, '. . . or if it's to further my education, then I have to refuse.'

'Who says that you'll learn more from me than I from you? The charity I am devoted to is myself. You will discover that soon enough. Your handwriting?' she asked, 'Is it presentable? If it is, you could write my letters for me, the report on my findings, descriptions of the things we encounter en route. I would entrust you with small personal matters. You could take care of them for me. But more than that, actually . . .' She looked at me. 'I would like to have you as a friend.'

4

How people can be moved by the sight of a ruin is a thing I'll have to get explained in the hereafter! What's so attractive about a heap of rubble? On our way south, Zélide insisted on stopping at every pile of stones she saw. After circling it, she could sit down beside it and drift off for hours. Meanwhile it was up to me to measure the debris, sketch it and mark its precise location on the map. Back in the carriage, Zélide would then insist on philosophising about the size and purpose of the buildings we had just seen.

'What buildings?' I sometimes grumbled. 'I didn't see any buildings, just grit.' This seemed to entertain her and encourage even more analyses of antique architecture, which lasted until we stumbled upon the next pile. Some days we only covered five or six miles in this fashion, after which it was my task to spend my whole evening at the inn rehashing her theories and writing them out neatly for her.

Somewhere near Pitigliano, a lump of cement set her to calculating the span of an enormous dome and the counter-thrust necessary to support it, even though we had not eaten all day and had miles to go to reach the next village.

'There isn't any dome!' I insisted, hungry and short-tempered.

'But there could have been.'

'And *that* might have been a delicious roast chicken,' I said, pointing to the faeces some shepherd or other had left between the rubble, 'but I'd rather see the original.'

'Not me,' she laughed and I began to suspect why the learned women in Bologna had never fully embraced her. 'If you show me a roast chicken, that's all there is to it. But if I see what's left of it, I am free to fantasise. The man who relieved himself here might not have had anything more than a piece of dry bread to eat, but in my imagination I give him a feast. The challenge is not seeing what *is*, but what might have been.'

Finally we reached Portici, where we were going to spend the autumn on the Bay of Naples in a simple apartment that had been placed at our disposal by a distant cousin of Zélide's late husband, Maria Amalia of Saxony, who had recently married the king of the Two Sicilies. While strolling through the grounds of the country house the king had built for their wedding, Maria Amalia had discovered a well into which the local townspeople regularly descended on ropes, coming back up a few hours later with antique coins and pins. At her insistence, her husband hired an antiquary to go down into the well. After passing through a system of underground tunnels, he discovered several marble steps, which he dug out and laid bare. It turned out to be the top of a Roman amphitheatre that lay buried under the soil.

By the time we visited it, the amphitheatre had been three-quarters excavated, together with the outbuildings. Sixty-foot deep, they could be reached down seven narrow ladders. For the long descent, Zélide ordered special, thin cotton skirts we could tie up like trousers. After reaching the bottom, we were led around by Marcello Venuti, who, together with his brothers, was in charge of the whole operation. Proudly, he wet a sponge and wiped the wall of the amphitheatre to show us the inscription; suddenly the letters stood out like new. The inscription declared that the city – the rest of it was apparently still hidden under the hill – was dedicated to the god Hercules. Venuti took this as proof that we were now standing in one of the cities which, according to the histories, had been buried under a layer of ash by an eruption of Vesuvius sixteen centuries before, soon after the death of Christ, and been considered lost for ever.

Zélide seemed unusually moved by this, especially when we walked around the outside of the theatre on an antique road. This section of street was exactly like the roads we know today, which you can see everywhere without having to carry out daredevil feats to get there. The Venuti brothers pointed out shops and small restaurants where the original pots and dishes still lay where they had been found. Bottles and cups on the counter of one of them made it look like a modern inn whose customers had only just left. This made such a deep impression on Zélide that she was quite overcome. The brothers took us to the adjoining basilica to recover. From the outside, only the bronze doors were visible, but they showed us in, brought us some cold water and left us alone for a while.

As my eyes adjusted to the gloom, I was able to make out more and more of the splendour around us. First to loom up in the diffuse light from the small star-shaped opening in the otherwise buried dome were two equestrian statues. Then I discovered the intricate, colourful patterns laid into the marble floor, the glimmering golden figures in the mosaics on the walls and, in the middle of the immense room, an enormous porphyry basin containing a pool of water deep enough to bathe in. The earth was like an oven. The air hung heavy under the arches. Our cotton garments clung to our bodies. I dabbed my face and chest, washed my wrists and ankles, and sprinkled the cool liquid over my hair. Then I did the same for my mistress until the cool water woke her from her reverie. She unbuttoned her blouse and bent over the basin to wash her upper body and armpits. Now and then her red hair flared in the light reflected on the water.

'Do you see now, Galatea,' she sighed, 'how everything is already present? Finished and complete. It exists, even if we're not aware of it. The fact that we don't notice something doesn't mean it isn't there.' She stretched and stood there for a moment with her arms up in the air, letting the draught in the subterranean chamber play over her damp body. 'Just as the earth conceals all these secrets within it, we too carry all the answers within us, even ones to questions we don't even know we can ask.'

As exuberant as a little girl, she suddenly ran up to me and grabbed my hands. 'Yes, today I am convinced, dear child! Our mind searches furiously for new knowledge but neglects the old. What does reason do with the innate understanding we sometimes have of things without being able to provide any hard evidence that it's true? Absolutely nothing! My learned friends would laugh at me if I drew their attention to it. They only believe things they can prove, but I say, "What about all the things whose existence we feel but cannot demonstrate?" '

I disentangled myself from her grip to take some quick notes as I was already starting to get lost and anticipated that it would be up to me to turn all these disconnected thoughts into a comprehensible whole that evening after dinner. Zélide, however, insisted on sweeping me up in her growing excitement.

'Reason is only the shell of consciousness. Under it, we have emotion. In our hearts, where no one can see us, we dare to trust it implicitly and know everything without words. If we never had to go out into the world, we would never doubt our intuition for a moment. But we do go out, and, when we do, we want our insides to be as presentable as the rest. We comb through our thoughts and straighten them up. Don't you remember, as a child, instinctively knowing what people were like, who would be good to you and who you should avoid, what you had to do to be fed, to survive and be loved? I believe that much of the knowledge we are seeking, the answer to all the important questions, has been present within us since our birth. We've simply forgotten how to tap into it. More than that, we've forgotten that most of it even exists. Just as people walked over this city for centuries without suspecting that it was here under their feet. All that intuitive knowledge is at its strongest at our birth, when we need it the most and have nothing else to draw on in our fight for survival. It lessens as we learn to think rather than feel, but it is never lost completely. It lies buried beneath the avalanche of argument and reasoning we need to understand today's world. Now and then, in the odd dream or while letting our thoughts wander, we might suddenly rediscover part of it. An artist would call it inspiration, for a believer it is revelation. But those of us who try to think rationally? Perhaps we would simply call it an idea, a moment of enlightenment in which you suddenly see the solution to a problem you have not yet formulated. These unexpected insights astonish us. We are so proud of having learned to think as individuals that we no longer wish to consider the possibility that we might once have been part of a greater whole. And I'm not even talking about the moments everyone has experienced, things like thinking of someone just before you bump into them or seeing a vision of a family member or loved one just before they exhale their last breath miles and miles away from wherever you happen to be. It's much simpler. Fragments of intuitive knowledge lie like shards on the surface of our being. The obvious thing to do after stumbling across one of these shards would be to dig deep within ourselves, but that's the one thing we don't do, because we can't grasp it with our intellect, and nowadays we're frightened of anything we're unable to explain rationally. Instead, we pick up our shard and slip it into our pocket in the hope that one day, by chance, we might discover another piece that fits it. In this way the scientific impulse impedes any view of our original knowledge, our intuition. It is buried, ever deeper, under the facts we gather during our lives; and the older we get and the more we learn, the more difficult it becomes to catch a glimpse of it.'

The Venuti brothers must have caught more than a glimpse when they suddenly arrived before Zélide and I had a chance to make ourselves decent. Unannounced, they appeared in the sun-drenched opening between the bronze doors, and we could only hope that their eyes still had to adjust to the gloom while we, with trembling hands, did up our garments and tamed our hair. Marcello was a stuffy scholar who looked like he had spent too much time underground, but Ridolfino and Filippo were in their prime. They were sunburnt and sweaty from digging. They had rolled up their shirt-sleeves and even the legs of their trousers. The mud was up to their thighs and the hair on their legs was plastered down like the fur of animals. Shamelessly, they kept their eyes fixed on those places where my wet dress revealed more of my body than decency allowed.

When they presented themselves freshly washed that evening to ask whether we would like to celebrate San Gennaro with them, I didn't hesitate for a moment. Cheerfully taking us by the hand, they pulled us out onto the terrace, where we could see the glow of fires lighting up the city on the other side of the bay, from the Castel dell'Ovo to Posillipo. But Zélide wouldn't come.

'Excellent,' I teased, 'then the gentlemen will have even more time for me,' but my mistress responded to this with such a profound silence that I immediately felt guilty. I offered to decline their offer after all, so that we could spend the evening like all our others, exchanging our thoughts and experiences and writing them down, but she wouldn't hear of it. She told me that I owed it to my youth, bid me enjoy myself, and promised that she herself would order and note down her thoughts about the day.

No one understands pleasure like the Neapolitans, and it was almost dawn by the time I returned home, drunk with success. As neither Ridolfino nor Filippo had been deterred by my disfigurement – perhaps because their work had accustomed them to the sight of damaged beauty – and the brothers were anything but shy with each other, I had experienced something in their arms that might have scared off a normal girl my age. But since my illness I had received no attention from young men at all, and before that I had only known my all-too-cautious Giacomo, so I abandoned myself completely to the bacchanalia, performing feats I might have thought physically impossible, if I had not seen illustrations of them in my *Dom Bougre*. The pleasure I experienced was something I felt not in my body but in my soul, and all the more intensely because of it. My soul seemed – I don't know how else to say it – so elevated by my shamelessness that it broke free from my body and looked down from a great height at the contortions below. More than anything else, I was deeply moved that I, of all people, was the object of the brothers' desire. This was possibly the only time I would ever arouse such great longing in handsome young men, and succeeding with both of them at once really was a tremendous joy. It brought me peace of mind. I forgot my imperfection. I stopped thinking and only felt. Yes, as long as they were pushing into me, I felt sure of myself. After our play was over, I didn't want to let my rapture subside and stoked it by gazing at the relaxation and childish gratitude on the faces of the brothers, who lay there recovering from their exertions with their heads on my belly.

Zélide was of course asleep by the time I came home with my head drooping, but the oil lamp she had left burning for me was still flickering on her writing table. Beside it lay the essay she had written while I was out dancing. I was so full of myself that I thought she had deliberately left it out like that to make me feel guilty about my idleness. I was stung that someone could resent my having a good time and, in my drunkenness, I was capable of waking her with reproaches, shouting that she was obviously too old and dried-out to remember how people of flesh and blood made love; that's how charged I was at that moment. Thank God, my curiosity was greater than my annoyance, and I flicked through a few pages of what she had written. To my surprise there were almost no observations of the places we had visited that day; instead, the essay was filled with echoes of our conversation in the basilica. Zélide elaborated her theory of the loss of intuitive knowledge during the development of the mind. The tone and content of her long meditation could not have been further from the banal emotional state in which I found myself at that moment. In every word, I recognised her over-sensitive soul and its reluctance to surrender to the inflexible regime of reason. At the same time, she spoke straight from her heart without trying to prove anything, not referring to any branch of science at all, but relying on her own experience. It was one of her best works. In a somewhat adapted form and expanded with two later dissertations on the same subject, it was eventually published in Nancy as *De l'origine du savoir* under her regular pseudonym, M. de M. I still own a copy. Another copy was added to the collection of the Bibliothèque du Roi on the recommendation of Monsieur Bignon of the Academy and can, to my knowledge, be consulted there to this day in the modern philosophy section.

As tired as I was, I read it in one sitting. The birds awoke. The sun came up. A sea breeze extinguished the oil lamp and carried the smell of ripe lemons in from the garden. My body and mind were so exhausted that they offered no resistance to ideas that I would surely have fought against otherwise. In my ecstatic state, I was scarcely able to separate the sensual delight that was still trembling within me from the passion of Zélide's words, although my weary head was incapable of following most of them.

Despite my exhaustion, I did not go to bed. Long after I had finished reading, I stayed sitting at the table. I felt empty. Even if my salvation had depended on it, I couldn't have got my body to move and my mind was frozen in the same way. I just sat there, will-less and empty-headed, staring out over the waves at the distant islands. Zélide came in and stood next to me. She didn't say a word about the essay lying in front of me. She only laid a hand on my shoulder. Then I began to cry – for the first time since Fate had marked me. For one and a half years, I had not shed a tear and now friendliness achieved what sorrow could not. I wept and wept. And all the while, Zélide and I stared out to sea without a word.

Zélide concludes her treatise 'On the Origin of Knowledge' by comparing our innate but undiscovered knowledge to the buried cities around Vesuvius, whose existence we never suspect until the day we happen upon an ancient street and walk on antique cobbles. If one exists, she argues, unnoticed for centuries and yet unchanged, then the other cannot be excluded. With this, she seems to have rounded off her argument. Then, suddenly, as an encore, in just a few sentences, she goes on to compare them both to love, which is just as impossible to prove rationally, but – sometimes long after being forgotten or given up as lost – always re-emerges as an incontrovertible presence: '*Each of us feels, after all, that he or she is capable of loving. We never doubt it and yet it is something that we have absolutely no certainty about until the day we find someone who is worthy of this gift.*'

'That's enough now,' said Zélide at last, drying my face. She ordered Turkish coffee and a hearty breakfast, which I couldn't bear the sight of: just the smell of freshly baked bread was enough to send the gall churning up my throat.

'I have seen enough of Naples and will be returning to Paris. If you have no other plans, you may remain in my service.'

As far as I knew, I had no plans at all, other than a firm resolution never to drink another drop of wine as long as I lived. I promised Zélide that I would stay with her, although at that moment I was seriously considering the possibility that my blood was so badly poisoned that I might succumb that very day. She picked an orange in the garden and peeled it for me, despite my assurances that I would not be able to swallow a bite.

'I cannot think of anything that would make me happier,' she whispered shyly, 'than to know that I can count on your friendship.' Whereupon she immediately risked losing it, by forcing a segment of orange on me. Then she ordered the servants to close the shutters, fluffed up the cushions and laid me down on the sofa to rest. She dabbed my forehead with a cool cloth until the hammering began to subside.

'It's agreed then,' she said, just when I thought my chances of pulling through had improved. 'You and I leave together for Paris. I'll write ahead telling them to prepare one of the rooms facing the garden for you. All new furnishings. There's plenty of time to get everything ready. On the way to Paris, we'll spend some time in Venice.'

I sat up cautiously, pressing my hands against my forehead

to try to stifle the echoes of the sledgehammer blow that had struck my brain.

'Venice?'

'Yes,' she beamed, 'six weeks or so at the most, I thought. Or would you rather stay longer?'

5

A dead dog was floating in the seaweed, its gut bloated with gases. Our gondolier pushed the animal out of the way with his paddle to moor the boat. Its skin burst open. Two pieces of hide stuck to the quayside. As we stepped ashore, they slapped against the stones under our feet.

After meeting Giacomo, I had tried to imagine what it would be like to live with him in this city, but realised that I had no clear image of it. The snatches of the countess's conversations I had caught as a child made it sound like a place of mystery, an enormous, open-air ballroom filled with ladies, thieves and doges, singers and actresses, a playground awaiting the day I would be old enough to enter it. Maybe I saw colour when I heard the name, lots of colours crowded together, I definitely saw people dancing and everywhere the glitter of sunlight and lamps on water, enormous palaces with lots of gold. Although . . . I had never actually seen a Venetian *palazzo*, so I imagined country homes like ours in Pasiano, but with their staircases and landings in the water, lined up and separated by beautiful parks. From the details in

Giacomo's stories, which I had listened to with my eyes closed and my head on his lap, I had put together a world of my own with quays and squares we strolled through arm in arm. The mansions in my dreams may not have resembled the real houses, but they had porticoes and courtyards that felt familiar and safe because my love was at home there and had played there as a child.

The moment I knew that I would never be his and his city would never be mine, that changed, and I had not given San Marco or the Grand Canal another thought. I had reconciled myself to never visiting the lagoon. And when they did come back to me against my wishes, the places Giacomo had described, I pushed them aside. With all the strength I had in me. Darkness took the place of light. Of course, not wanting to think about something does not mean that we no longer carry an image of it with us. It just loses its radiance and becomes grey and tarnished. Before, the sun was shining in through the stained glass; now the sky is overcast. There, where everything was bright and colourful, you suddenly see ungainly welds in the lead and pigeon shit on the panes.

The reality was much worse: the sludge on the bridges, the piles of refuse in the alleys, the smell of sweaty bodies milling together, the rats at the rubbish . . . The stench of the fish market hung over the Rialto. The steps were littered with dead birds, their necks wrung by the maize vendors. Everywhere, screams and curses rose up from packed streets. The crowd knotted together in the *sottoportegi*. People elbowed you in the side trying to get past. In front of the churches, beggars pushed their festering stumps into your face.

'Enchanting,' Zélide sighed, 'the way the people here have stayed themselves without the slightest concession to modern comforts! Here, at least, they appreciate life because they have to fight each other for every breath of fresh air. Imagine that in the Tuileries!'

Her curiosity about the seamy side of life went so far that I wouldn't have put it past her to check in for the night at an inn full of tanners; thank God, she had already rented an apartment in the Palazzo Cini. As soon as we stepped through the door, the filthy city around us seemed to dissolve. Thick walls muffled the cries, heavy drapes kept out the smoke and the stench, and all the rooms were fitted with an ingenious ventilation system that provided a fresh sea breeze at the tug of a cord. Here I entrenched myself. Once a day we crossed the canal to the Piazzetta to visit the library. Sometimes we took a boat to San Lazzaro to see the Indian miniatures and Egyptian manuscripts that are kept there under the guard of Armenian monks. Beyond this, I accompanied Zélide on short, purposeful excursions to places where I could be sure not to bump into Giacomo: her seamstress's workshop or the bathhouse. At the latter, I managed to relax a little. Zélide had chosen one not far from the ghetto, in Cannaregio, which was mainly used by ordinary women from the neighbourhood. A few times a week we hired an enclosed gondola to go there and spent one or two hours hidden in the warm mist, while an elderly Ottoman masseuse rubbed us with oils. On these precious afternoons we sat silently together, our minds blank. Generally we dined at home, and if we had received an invitation to go somewhere or if Zélide wanted to go to the *ridotto* to enjoy herself, I would think of some excuse to stay at home. When she entertained guests in the apartment, I pleaded illness and stayed in bed. Behind the windows of my room, which were tall and narrow like the windows of a chapel, the city lay in a blue haze or trembled in the burning sun, but it was always far enough away for me to tell myself that it was just a mirage or a feverish delirium that would soon pass.

But it was always there. Tempting. Lying in wait. If I heard people laughing on the water, I began to believe that it was my cowardice they were laughing at. Worse still: when I heard a voice like his – and there were dozens of times every day when I thought the moment had come – I had to force myself not to rush to the window. I was torn. Hoping to forget the pain in my soul, I pressed my nails into my flesh until it bled. It was futile. The more I tried to block it out, the more vividly I imagined that somewhere out there, on the squares around the markets, lying between the vegetable peel and off-cuts, some remnant of my happiness must have survived.

Just when I thought I would lose my mind for ever if I did not leave the city immediately, salvation arrived. The theatres reopened. When an elated Zélide came home with costumes for the gala opening and a receipt for the rental of a box at the Teatro Chrisostomo, I did not immediately recognise the solution that had been tossed into my lap. I refused, of course, because if there was one place where I could be sure of bumping into Giacomo, an event like that, where he could meet people who could further his career, would be it. It wasn't until Zélide put on her costume and came to show it to me, donning her three-cornered hat and mask in the process, that it finally sank in: from October to mid-December, for the duration of the theatre season, the people of Venice are free to walk around masked. I could move amongst them without being seen. It might even be my chance to observe Giacomo again from close by, assuring myself that he was happy, maybe even seeing who he was with and whether the career he craved had begun to take shape. Zélide, who had no idea of the phantoms that had plagued me in the preceding weeks, was delighted with the revival in my sprits. She strapped me into the costume she had ordered for me, tied all the bows and pinched my breasts until they flushed – just as I did for her when she was going out. For me, she had chosen a *moretta*, a black leather mask you hold in place with a button between your teeth. This wasn't secure enough for me. I was afraid that, in my nervousness, I would drop it, revealing my identity after all, but Zélide didn't hesitate to swap. As a result, I wore the more beautiful of the two masks. It was made of white velvet and had small diamonds around the eyes. My only concern was that it should cover my whole face and that I should be able to pin it to my hair so that I could be confident it wouldn't fall off, even during the wildest dance.

I didn't see Giacomo. Or the performance. I couldn't take my eyes off the crowd in the auditorium and the corridors. Actually not a soul paid the slightest bit of attention to what was happening on the stage – some divertissement or other about Marco Polo, a hero of the republic who had been born on the site of this theatre. They were all too busy reconquering or, preferably, improving their position for the new season. The Countess of Montereale had not ex-aggerated when describing these evenings to me in Pasiano. Few moments were as propitious for improving one's fortune as the start of the season, and everyone was busy trying to outdo everyone else. Drawing attention to oneself now with conspicuous beauty or wealth, by making a witty comment or by spreading a vicious rumour, would arouse the interest of the others for months to come and guarantee admission to all the soirées. Inversely, one flaw, a single faux pas or a slip of the tongue, would be enough to squander all the favour one had amassed over the previous year. This is why the Venetians wear masks. Outsiders think otherwise, but there is nothing playful or festive about it. Concealing one's identity and choosing when and where to reveal it is the only way of escaping the constant, suffocating surveillance. Often it's a matter of life and death. A man who disgraces himself in public loses everything and has only two alternatives: suicide or exile. Only by flatly denying his identity and insisting that people's suspicions of the face behind the mask are misplaced can he avert the scandal and prevent the worst. His reputation will probably be ruined anyway, but he might save his life.

In a sense it reassured me to see with my own eyes how obsessed people in this city were about appearances; I had been right to give up Giacomo. He would have been ruined within a day of my disfigurement's becoming known. This knowledge made me even more curious about his career. The greater his success, the more justified my sacrifice. And if that lessened my regret, who knows, perhaps the sorrow that had been stirred up by staying in this city would also be diminished.

That evening, however, there was no sign of him. I worried that he might not have attained any status at all in the intervening years. I plucked up my courage and began to ask round about the young *Abbé* Casanova. The name seemed unfamiliar to most people and only three turned out to know him: one said that Giacomo had served for a time as a soldier in Fort Sant' Andrea; another that he had gone to Rome to try his luck there; and, according to number three, he was either on Corfu or in the hands of the mufti of Constantinople, the Turkish pope. As none of them knew anything for certain, I tried not to let them worry me.

Then I saw Adriana! She was there with her husband and a few friends. I had already rushed up to her and was standing breathless before her, when I realised from the astonished look in her eyes that she could not possibly recognise me. With a shock, I also realised that if she saw Giacomo regularly, as I hoped, she would certainly tell him of my presence in the city if I revealed my identity. I decided to remain anonymous, exchanged a few courtesies and then raised all the nonchalance I could muster to ask about the young *abbé* she had invited to her wedding. On hearing his name, she laughed a little, as if many others had asked before me. She had not seen Giacomo for some time, but gave me the address of his brother, Francesco, who was now studying theatre architecture. Adriana knew him well because he earned a living as an artist and had painted a number of murals of naval battles for her. Keeping our exchange short and businesslike, I said goodbye immediately, even though I would gladly have given a year of my life to talk to her about Monsieur de Pompignac and reminisce together about the summers in Pasiano, her dear mother and my own parents.

The next morning I plucked up my courage and astonished Zélide by going out masked and alone around midday. I took the *traghetto* to the church of San Samuele, behind which I soon found the large house where Giacomo had lost his father. He had described it so lovingly that I felt like I already knew it: the sculpted angel above the door, the Moresque staircase with steps that were much too high, the marble lion's head at the top that had been worn down because everyone strokes the mane in passing. On the *piano nobile* I found Francesco in his studio. One wall was covered with a large canvas on which he had depicted the battle of Lepanto. Scale-models of stage sets he had designed were everywhere, along with innumerable walnut and rosewood models of the most ingenious landings and spiral staircases, some no larger than a thumb, others as tall as a man. He sat between them sketching. I pretended that I was thinking of commissioning him and looked around. Just as I had rehearsed at home, I asked about prices and ideas for a ceiling painting. I sounded much braver than I felt, but he saw right through me.

'It's about my brother, isn't it?'

'What makes you think that?'

'People visited Tintoretto in his studio. When someone wants *me* to paint something, he sends for me. If I'm not at his door within the hour, he gets someone else. The only people who bother to come here are hideous old usurers I owe money to and beautiful young women who ask about Giacomo. You're out of luck. He's gone abroad.'

'I bet you say that to all the girls.'

He laughed.

'This time it's true.'

Francesco squinted, as if to draw my portrait, and stared at me so brazenly that I couldn't help but feel my mask to make sure it hadn't slipped.

'Haven't we met somewhere before?' he asked.

'I don't think so.'

'There's something about the way you hold yourself . . .'

I sat down. After bringing me a drink, Francesco laid a letter on the table in front of me. He himself took a sheet of paper and began sketching to give me an opportunity to read at my leisure. The letter was from Giacomo, addressed to his brother and sent recently from Turkey. The tone was laddish, very different from how I remembered him and not pleasant to me at all. He described using sleight of hand to swindle a dragoman; learning to smoke a hookah with *zamanda* tobacco; and not being allowed to set foot anywhere without being accompanied by a janissary, who showed him a harem, laughed at his ignorance concerning the morals of Muslim women, and tutored him on that same subject. Giacomo went on to joke about the fact that these women would rather bare their bodies to him than their faces, which had to remain hidden by law.

'He tends to make it sound more beautiful than you or I might,' Francesco explained when I replaced the letter without reading it to the end. 'He doesn't mean it badly. He has just resolved to enjoy life, and if a day passes without his experiencing something that seems special enough, he simply embellishes. It's nothing to get upset about.'

'No,' I said. 'Why should anyone get upset about that?'

I then asked Francesco to tell me more about his brother's general well-being. It seemed that his career was not proceeding as rapidly as he might have wished. Still, for someone of such humble origins, he had managed with his charm and erudition quickly to gain the confidence of a number of influential people, both within the republic and in the Vatican, and the signs were all favourable for his return.

'And love?' I wanted to ask. 'Have his qualities helped him to prosper in that area as well?' I didn't dare and stood up to leave.

'And as far as his loves are concerned . . .' said Francesco. Without finishing his sentence, he laid the drawing he had sketched while I was reading Giacomo's letter on the table and turned it around so I could see it properly.

'Very skilful,' I said, 'who is it meant to be?'

My dress, my hair, my posture, all perfectly rendered. He had drawn everything except my mask. In its place he had drawn the unblemished face I once had, the face he remembered from his visit to Pasiano and assumed I must still have. I didn't flinch, but studied the portrait politely and slid it away without showing any further interest.

'And his loves?'

'He has them.'

'I'm glad.'

'In all shapes and sizes.'

'My,' I said, turning away to escape the gaze that was still fixed on me. I stood close to the naval battle and studied it as if I were an expert.

'He nets them one after the other, and sometimes a brace at a time.'

The waves were red with blood. The Turkish fleet was shattered. A commander was drowning between the oars of one of the Serenissima's triremes. His turban had come undone and trailed on the water like a long golden ribbon.

'Why do you think that would be?' Francesco asked in a hostile voice.

'Pardon?'

'What, do you think, could have made him so insatiable, that brother of mine?'

'I . . . I really have no idea.'

'No?'

'No, but I know that I am grateful that he, at least, does not suffer from a lack of love.'

'Is that so?'

I was standing so close to the enormous canvas that it trembled on its stretcher – a small ripple spread across the wall. I braced myself to say goodbye, but Francesco continued in that same reproachful tone.

'They never last long, these fancies of his. A single night, a few at the most, then the next one has already caught his eye.'

'From the look on your face, one would think that a young man must suffer terribly from something like that.'

'Not him. On the contrary. That way he always keeps one step ahead of his disappointment. He's learnt his lesson.'

Now I really wanted to leave and walked out. Francesco followed, holding the drawing he had done of me. He hesitated awkwardly, as if he wanted to give it to me but was too shy. He held it up.

'So you don't know her?'

I shook my head. Then he ripped the portrait into pieces and threw them into the canal. They spread out over the water.

'By all that is sacred to me, I don't know anyone who looks like that.'

The paper grew heavy. The ink ran.

6

Slowly everything dissolved. Outlines grew dim. The mist scattered the light, making everything seem less sharp. I caught an occasional glimpse of a naked, gleaming body and heard sighs or gurgling water in the distance. Otherwise, I was able to feel alone. My thoughts relaxed. The steam forced its way in, and they fell apart like a sugarloaf in water. They didn't disappear, but at last they began to move, growing softer and smoother. They seemed lighter, if only because they were no longer knotted together. They drifted apart, as if the anxiety was spreading out over my whole body instead of bearing down on my stomach. Sometimes a blast of hot breath burst through the mist and Zélide loomed up. She was sitting opposite me and every now and then she blew aside the white curtain that hung between us to let me know she was still there and make sure I was all right.

When I had returned to the Palazzo Cini after my excursion – agitated and self-reproachful because my wretched curiosity had led to my discovering more than I wanted to know – Zélide was standing in front of the house on the small bridge to the Campo San Vio as if waiting for me. She took off my mask. One glance was enough. She understood without asking a single question. Without knowing what had happened, she followed her natural impulse, like a mother who comforts her son when he has fallen, not by wailing and stroking the injury, but simply by feeling his pain and distracting him with her empathy. Calm, but brooking no objections, she packed me into a gondola and took me to the baths in Cannaregio. There she undressed me, washed me all over, wrapped me in a sheet, took me by the hand and led me into the steam room. I shrank back into a corner on one of the stone benches and wrapped my arms around my knees.

I sat there.

'Shame is one of the basest of urges,' said Zélide. 'I place it at the bottom of the ladder of civilisation, between revenge and jealousy. It's a destructive force and fed by fear.' I heard her from close by, but could not see her. 'We carry this dangerous tendency within us as one of nature's burdens, but we must fight against it. We must!'

There she was. Her face suddenly close to mine.

'What is it?' She was staring at me. I felt uncomfortable.

'It's no challenge to see what *is* . . .' she whispered. I looked her in the eyes. I don't believe we had ever been so close before. A few drops of water ran down her forehead. One hung from her nose. 'Don't you want to fight it, Galatea? Shame? Please. It's not too late. I'll help you if you like.' She took my hand and squeezed it encouragingly. 'If it's so easy for me to see what *was*, don't you think that others will be able to see it as well?'

She moved away again, opening a trail through the clouds to lie down on the bench across from mine. Turning her back on me, she stretched and groaned with relaxation.

'That's why I love being naked. I love it even more with other people than I do when I'm alone. Don't you feel that?

Especially with others! Daring to take such liberties is a triumph over our nature.'

After this it was quiet for so long that I thought she must have dozed off. The mist thickened. Then I heard her turning over, her damp skin sticking to the smooth stone.

'Really, chastity is only something for the lowest class. Those kind of people are uneducated and frightened. They need rules and prohibitions to make sense of their world. In the better circles, it's quite unknown. I have yet to visit a court that was very particular about chastity.'

I could do it. Really, I could. What was the chance of this much friendship ever coming my way again? I undid the sheet and laid it to one side. I blew hard a few times until she came into sight, then let her calmly feast her eyes on what she had desired for so long. We blew the hot air back and forth to ensure that nothing came between us.

She was already sick. The poison gnawed away at her from the inside, so that her appearance remained the same until the end, and for a long time I did not suspect a thing. She kept her pain from me as long as she could, afraid that I would seek another position. I stayed in her service for four more years. All that time we lived in Vincennes. The first months were a constant celebration. For days on end we wandered through Paris together.

With typical French pride, Zélide showed me the wonders of her city. She was popular in the most scintillating circles. We visited scores of scholars and magistrates who were anxious to hear about her journey and her discoveries near Naples. Wherever we went, she introduced me as an equal, the bosom friend she was so keen to have. As a consequence people expected me to participate in discussions of all manner of subjects, and I learnt to converse in the French style, which requires one to handle words and arguments like a juggler, keeping them in the air for as long as possible.

When the haemorrhaging began and Zélide had to take to bed, she refused to allow anyone else to nurse her. This decline lasted more than three years. In the end I laid her out and buried her myself. There was a will in which I was named. The bulk of her fortune had been eaten up by her investigations, 'wasted' as the notary put it. The remainder passed by law to the children of her deceased husband. To me, she left all the metal and glass apparatus that she had accumulated in her years of experimentation. The stable and the coach-houses were full of them. It took me three months just to draw up an inventory. In the end I found a coppersmith who was willing to buy the lot for five louis d'or, just enough to keep me for two months.

The weaker she grew, the more desperately Zélide clung to 'science', although it became less and less clear what this actually meant to her. More and more often, her unwillingness to place reason above emotion led to vague enthusiasms and irrational interests. These she pursued with an insistence that only alienated her further from her friends and acquaintances. She plunged into the wildest of enterprises as if they offered some chance of a cure. At the same time science was becoming so fashionable in Europe and the number of fields in which new discoveries were being made was expanding so rapidly, that everyone seemed to be involved in it and it grew increasingly difficult to separate serious thinkers from quacks and showmen. Many of these frauds profited from Zélide's gullibility and, even when she saw through them, she sometimes continued to fund them because, as her end approached, clinging to a dream seemed much more important than facing up to reality.

Although I did my best to separate the wheat from the chaff, giving numerous charlatans a kick in the pants at the door, Zélide abandoned herself to countless whims that cheered her so much I couldn't bring myself to deprive her of them. One was her obsession with horseless transport. To this end, she acquired from the Papin heirs the original plans for a steamship, which she intended to build on the Marne. To generate enough steam, the vessel would have needed to carry so much wood that there would have been almost no room for the crew, let alone freight, but that did not bother her at all. She brought an engineer over from England to explain the workings of Newcomen's steam pump, an enormous machine with gigantic pistons and cylinders that was already half a century old and had been long discarded as impossible. When neither Meyer's Dutch steam engine nor a pneumatic pump produced the desired results, Zélide had the salon cleared to set up a machine that produced static electricity with the help of a so-called Leyden jar. This was a terrifying spectacle which attracted half of Paris. For weeks on end, we received guests and demonstrated the phenomenon until Zélide shut her doors for good, incensed that her visitors were only interested in the entertainment value of an innovation that she suspected would one day be a boon to humanity. Frustrated by her inability to harness the electricity she could see with her own eyes and, even worse, unable to provide any reasonable proof or explanation of it, she surrendered the last critical capacities she had left. *Observo, ergo est* became her creed: if she could see it, it was true. This cleared the way for a broad range of confidence men, who succeeded in arousing her enthusiasm for all kinds of things, simply by providing plausible demonstrations. These included a young man from Neuchâtel who built androids, mechanical puppets that could write, compose and play chess; the 'Count of Saint Germain', who proved the effectiveness of his elixir of life by relating how he himself, as an acquaintance of Jesus, had witnessed His miracles in Canaan; and a doctor who promised to treat Zélide's illness by means of tyromancy, the practice of reading the future from a piece of cheese.

★

First she involved me in all her experiments, but soon she had retreated too far into her own world to share it with me. My scepticism disturbed her. Our conversations became less personal, and in the end I was able to help her more as a servant than I could as a friend. She had my support when she wanted it and was free to ignore my advice – which I continued to give her, even as a subordinate. In this way we both lived satisfactory lives without annoying each other too much. It was only in the last few weeks that our conversations regained their old intimacy. By then, she was permanently confined to bed but working harder than ever on a drawing board, which she always kept within reach. On it, she designed airships, one after the other, as many as three or four a day, and each one with a different shape, principle and operation.

She had come up with this idea not long before, after we had seen a fish surface in the pond in the courtyard by gulping air. It filled its body until it was quite round, then floated effortlessly. Once it had had enough, it let the air escape and sank to the bottom again. 'If this principle works in water,' Zélide said suddenly, 'why not outside it?' She became convinced that working from this assumption would lead her to the discovery that would cause her to be remembered for centuries, if only she had enough time left to develop the concept. Anyone else would have approached the matter practically and rationally, by first formulating the laws which governed the principle, but Zélide, who could hear the ticking of the clock, was in too much of a hurry and skipped that stage. After all, her emotions told her that she was on the right track. That was enough for her, and to avoid wasting any time, she went straight to dreaming about the applications of her new invention. She produced big colourful sheets, scribbled full with springs, cogs and puzzling formulae. Any technical principles that might have been present disappeared at crucial moments behind mind-boggling patterns or colourful balloons. The crew of the flying ships *was* worked out in detail. The aviators wore neat uniforms and the passengers leant over the railings.

If I annoyed her by asking how her machines could ever take off, she reacted as if stung. 'That's secret!' she replied, refusing to tell me any more than that they would be driven by what she called *soupe*. This liquid was activated by another, even more mysterious, fluid. The latter, green in colour, needed to be mixed with water before being dripped – an illustration depicted the process – onto hot coals to produce a pink gas that simply lifted the machines off the ground. I assumed that the disease had now reached her brains and was eating them away from the inside. To look at, she was as beautiful as ever, but she was feverish, and I decided to torment her no longer with reality.

The moments of clarity never ceased altogether. Then she would cry as if she had lost her way during a journey. In those hours I sat beside her like a mother with a daughter.

'What will you do?' she asked once.

'I'll tell the cook to make some broth and then we'll try to eat some of it together.'

'Not now!' She snapped at me because there was no time for trivialities. 'Later. When I'm not here any more, what will you do then?'

'What won't I do is a better question!' My frivolous tone backfired, and for a moment she seemed about to sink into melancholy.

'Perhaps that's the worst,' she mumbled softly to herself. 'Yes, the worst is that everything goes on and I shall never know how it ends.'

'Don't worry about me. The whole world is before me. Anything could happen. I'll find out in due course.'

Zélide tried to sit up straight. I helped her and fluffed up the pillows. Suddenly she grabbed me urgently by the wrist.

'A person can weigh up an infinite number of different

possibilities, but among them there is always one he wants the most. Remember that!'

I promised that I would, but my tone annoyed her. She heard the kindness in my voice – I had used it often these last few days in an attempt to soothe her and avoid any awkwardness. This time she refused to be placated and briefly recovered her old passion.

'Reason offers us many possibilities. Intuition infallibly chooses the best. If you remember this, you cannot err and you will always make the right choice.'

'Always?'

'Always!'

'Even in affairs of the heart?'

'Most of all! Don't be silly. It's so simple and yet people can spend a whole life without seeing it. Listen: it's a question of closing your eyes and doing the first thing that comes to mind. Do you hear me? That's all there is to it. A person is only ever capable of wanting one thing at a time.'

We sat for a long time hand in hand. This was our farewell. We both knew it. Even though she lived on for days afterwards, this was the moment in which we let go of each other without saying a word. When I finally stood up to get the broth, I gave her another kiss, but she had already picked up her drawing board and resumed work on one of her airships. With her tongue sticking out between her teeth, she sketched a married couple, passengers, drinking tea among the clouds at an outboard table. Zélide wrote beside it that it should be set with damask and real silverware.

That whole year, '49, had been unusually warm. In August it became unbearable. The days were scorching and the nights brought almost no relief. Leaving Vincennes I took just a few books and the clothes I could wear, but even before reaching the highway I was forced to take off the top layer and abandon it under a bush.

I was twenty years old, without family or loved ones, and with no more baggage than the lessons Zélide and Monsieur de Pompignac had taught me. Now that they had both died, it was clear that neither her exaltation nor his reasoning had made either of them any happier. I was free to take any road I wished. Years before, when leaving Pasiano, I had headed south. This time I chose the opposite direction.

I had set my heart on Amsterdam. The city's name was one of the first that Monsieur de Pompignac had taught me. I saw it many times in the books he gave me to read, the most important of which had all been printed in Holland, the place, he told me, where both Descartes and Spinoza had found refuge. Now and then, almost in awe, he opened a title page, showed me the name of the printer and praised the Dutch for their intellectual freedom. He told me that the Hollanders were clean and tolerant, prosperous and Christian; they were convinced of the equality of all people and would never stop anyone from expressing an opinion. They traded all over the world, importing not just pepper and coffee, but also the beliefs of other nations. Men like Locke and Bayle had found sanctuary there and praised the climate that permitted them to move and think freely. From Signora Manzolini's library in Bologna, I knew the *Systema Naturae* and the *Genera Plantarum* with all the flowers and species that Linnaeus had studied in Amsterdam's Botanical Gardens. I only had to think of that city to see before me a paradise where, amid all the flowers of the world, the liberated human spirit and all the branches of science blossomed.

The trees along the road from Vincennes to Paris had been pruned in the latest style. They provided hardly any shade and the birds struggled – beaks open and wings spread – to survive beneath them. I searched in vain for a carriage that could take me to the Marais, where coaches left for the north. Even before I had covered the first of the six miles to the city, I was drenched with sweat. When I came to the bridge over the stream I did not hesitate for a moment, but descended and refreshed myself with the cool water under its dark arches. Then I put on the minimum of clothes to remain respectable, folding my petticoat into a pouch so that I could carry some of the others. When I climbed back up to the road, I saw a man approaching. He was immersed in whatever he was reading. He didn't look up or around and had come within ten steps of me when he suddenly froze. He shrieked and reached for his head as if he had been hit by a rock, but it can only have been the overwhelming impact of the words he had just read. He gasped for breath like a wounded man and flailed around as if looking for something to hold on to. I ran up and helped him to sit down. When I spoke, he did not respond. I assumed that it was sunstroke and hurried off to fetch some water, but when I returned he was too elated to drink.

'It's true though, isn't it?' he shouted, grabbing both my hands as if he wanted to dance around in a circle with me. 'What kind of curiosity is it that wants to know exactly how things work? Calculations are motivated by greed, and without injustice, there would be no need to study law! Imagine: without wars and conspiracies, no history!'

On this he burst into tears. I realised that he was in a worse state than I had thought and tried to disentangle myself. When the fellow saw how frightened I was, he apologised as best he could.

'Please excuse me, I was going to Vincennes . . . My friend,' he blurted. 'He's imprisoned there. I'm on my way to visit him, and I read . . . I could have taken any book, but this morning I chose this, by chance. Isn't it incredible? And I read . . . By chance, I suddenly read this here.' Unable to go on, he pressed the *Mercure de France* into my hands and pointed out an advertisement. I seized the opportunity to escape and left him behind by the side of the road, still dazed.

Only later, when I had secured a seat in a coach and we were heading north at a trot, did I read the advertisement that had had such an impact on the lunatic. It was an announcement by the Academy of Dijon of an essay competition. The theme of the treatise was provided: *Has the progress of science and the arts contributed to the deterioration or to the improvement of moral behaviour?* No idea, but whatever else it's done, it hasn't made it any safer on the streets. It is simply ghastly how many madmen you bump into these days. Grateful to have escaped such an encounter unscathed, I mumbled a prayer. I threw the paper out of the open window of the coach, but until Senlis at least I was pursued by a vague sadness. It was most like the impotence I felt one night as a little girl in Pasiano when I heard the adults outside on the terrace. Their tone of voice told me that they were discussing something exciting that was tremendously important, but no matter how hard I tried, I was unable to make out enough of their conversation to work out what it was.

III

Theatrum Amatorium

Every autumn my parents spent a week or two at my uncle's farm in Belluno. Boar were more common there than in Pasiano, and the deer seemed less wary. What's more, my parents explained, the partridges gathered in the open fields and flew straight at the hunters. While my father was off hunting with his brother, my mother and her sister-in-law went out looking for blackberries, red currants and mushrooms. At midday everyone came together to butcher and salt the game, clean and dry the mushrooms, and cook and preserve the fruit.

The fun we had when my parents came back always made up for how sad I felt while they were away. They unpacked their heavily laden bags in the kitchen, lined up the delicacies we would be eating until spring, and let me taste the candied walnuts and the red currant jelly. Until I grew too old to believe them, my mother would tell me stories about my uncle and aunt, and how they lived on a candy mountain in the Land of Cockaigne, next to a lake of wine.

The autumn after I turned six, my parents decided that I

was big enough to go with them. The mountain turned out to be hidden under a thick forest and the lake next to the small farm was covered with a black layer of rotting leaves. My uncle and aunt were simple people. They had one son, Geppo, who they loved heart and soul. He was about ten years older than me and retarded. Ever since he was little they had kept him chained up in their yard. When we headed off into the forest in the morning to gather all those delicacies, we heard my cousin, who wanted to come with us, straining at his chain in the distance. His mother was desperate to go back to comfort her child and had to steel herself to keep going, but at the same time they didn't dare to let the boy wander free: they were terrified that something might happen to him. At midday we put the big table near the simpleton and set to work, and our activity seemed to entertain him. Sometimes he sat down next to us and helped sort the nuts.

On warm days they let him go for a swim. That was his passion. He could race through the water for hours on end without resting. Broadly built and powerful, he seemed inexhaustible in his element. Still, they never let him go into the water without a strong rope tied around his waist. My uncle held the other end at all times, and when he felt an unexpected tug because his son had dived too deeply or swum too far from the shore, he would rush to rescue his child, even though my cousin was by far the better swimmer and had never once been in any danger.

The first two years I hardly dared to approach Geppo alone, but in the autumn that followed I got to know him better. I had twisted my ankle on a rocky path and had to stay behind when the others went into the woods. One morning, out of boredom, I hopped into the yard to look at my crazy cousin. He beckoned me and tried to grab my leg. When I let him take it, he turned out to have a gentle touch. For at least an hour, he massaged my foot and my swollen ankle, devoting himself completely to the task as if nothing else existed in the entire world, and by the time he was finished, I could stand without pain.

After that we became good friends. I chatted away to him, telling him about Pasiano and our lives there, the countess and her guests. At the end of the first week, Geppo suddenly interrupted me. I was shocked because it was the first time I had heard him speak, but I could understand what he was saying, even though his own words made him laugh uncontrollably at the end of every sentence and it was usually impossible to work out exactly what he was referring to.

We played together all of the following week, and when he was allowed to swim, I swam with him until he wore me out. At some stage I sighed about how terrible it was of his parents to keep him chained up. As usual, he didn't react, and I had talked to him about other things for at least an hour before he broke me off in mid-sentence.

'Yes,' Geppo exclaimed in a loud, clear voice, 'they love me because my head is poor.' At this he laughed so hard, he started coughing. When he had recovered, he added, 'That shows them how rich *their* heads are.'

When we arrived in Belluno the next year, my uncle and cousin were dead. They had drowned one day in summer when Geppo's rope got snagged on a branch while he was diving to the bottom of the lake. It held the boy down first, and then, when my uncle tried to rescue his son, he got tangled up in it as well. That autumn my father went hunting alone while my mother and I stayed with my aunt. She kept up a brave face in front of me and only once did I see her cry. My mother cooked the red currants, I sugared them and my aunt mashed them through a steel sieve. Her sorrow was silent, but suddenly I saw big round tears falling into the pulp.

'I was given so much,' she said to no one in particular. 'Surely it would have been ungrateful not to seize that happiness with both hands?' Then she awoke from her reverie, saw me sitting beside her and embraced me so passionately that I was left with mashed fruit in my hair. That was all she ever showed me of her grief, but that winter, when we went to draw on our supply of redcurrant jelly, you could taste the salt in every pot.

I

Amsterdam 1758

The women sit on low chairs and try to keep their backs to the public. They hold their heads down and their shoulders up, afraid of being hit with a hard object. They would do better to turn around, so that they could see when an attack was imminent and where it might be coming from, but the looks the visitors give them hurt more than any projectiles. Officially, throwing things at the prisoners is no longer permitted, but it remains the traditional highlight of this entertainment and the doorkeeper is willing, for a small surcharge on top of the admission fee, to let people bring in harmless objects for this purpose. Between the balls of paper and the vegetable peel, the visitors often conceal green apples or worse. They want value for money, and nothing beats the fun of making a whore yelp. Anyone who succeeds in drawing blood becomes an instant hero to the rest of the crowd. They even hold competitions and bet on who will manage it first. As if they haven't noticed any of this, the women on display remain bent over their work.

Like similar institutions in Delft, Leyden and The Hague,

the Amsterdam spin-house is a source of entertainment to the general public. Admission costs just two stivers and visitors can stay as long as they like. There are always a few overgrown youths who hope to impress their fiancées by cursing and insulting the prisoners, because oddly enough some wenches respond favourably to that kind of thing. The prison is also recommended in all the travel journals, so that no foreigner leaves Amsterdam without experiencing this particularly Dutch attraction.

'Incredible,' laughed Mr Jamieson, 'to think you've never been here before. You only live round the corner!' He spoke without taking his eyes off the women on show and failed to notice my discomfort. 'Where else in the world could you find an exhibition like this?' He then asked me what methods were used to force the women to reform and how one could tell which prisoners were thieves and which were whores, as they were all equally ugly in his eyes.

Mr Jamieson thought he was amusing me.

In the last few months, we had sought out a great deal of entertainment together in Amsterdam, invariably of the most innocent and light-hearted variety. He is a kind-hearted man who is undemanding and capable of enjoying the simple things of life. For years he did his own hunting, skinning and tanning, work that left him with rough manners and hands that scratch like pumice stones. But his fur and suede are famous, he says, and worn at all the courts of Europe, thanks to a secret technique that allows him to smooth out every irregularity, down to the smallest capillaries. He has held a monopoly over bear and beaver hunting in the valleys of the Hudson for several years and arrived in Holland in late summer with the plan of securing his European distribution from this basis.

We were seeing each other, as I mentioned, every Thursday. He would arrive in the afternoon and we would go for a walk together and dine somewhere. Sometimes we would go dancing as well or visit a soirée. We had never agreed to meet on this regular basis, it was simply a habit that developed naturally. When – on the evening that Fate decided to play tricks on me – he was unable to come because of gout, I was genuinely disappointed and spent a long time moping around as if the day had lost its purpose. Finally, I called myself to task – after all, Jamieson is twenty years older, unattractive and in no way a suitable match – and decided to spruce myself up and go to the French theatre. Whatever else it brought, that day showed me how much I loved the little outings Jamieson thought up for me and the way he whisked me off, chuckling with anticipation.

I had no reason at all to think that his new surprise might be so unpleasant. He called for me up at home. We weren't going far so walked out onto the Oudezijds Achterburgwal. When he stopped after just a few houses it was too late. He looked down at me with a beaming smile and gestured at the grand façade of the spin-house.

In the attic, where the whores and any other women who need to be put in their place are exhibited in a large cage, I explained things truthfully to Jamieson, who insisted that I tell him everything I knew about this institution. I did it in a terse, measured voice, because his sympathetic gasps annoyed me and I didn't want the women to hear them.

When I had finished my explanation, we fell as silent as the women themselves, who refuse to speak in the presence of an audience. Their punishment no longer consists of spinning, but of sewing linen. Most of them have bandaged fingers, because the thread abrades their flesh so deeply that it can sometimes expose and cut through tendons. For a while all we heard was the sound of hands working skilfully, fabric gliding through fingers and the occasional whipping sound of a sheet being folded with short, fierce gestures.

This wasn't enough for the other spectators. One of them whooped that if the whores were going to keep quiet, he wanted his two stivers back. Another supported him by shouting that their sisters on the street were a lot less lazy – in the alleys off the Kalverstraat they'd lend you 'a helping hand' for the same price. At this, the couple that watched over the fallen women's work and earnings, the house father and mother, came into action, admonishing the women to show themselves more openly by poking them in the side with sticks. Most of them submitted and turned reluctantly to face us, whereupon even more abuse was flung at them by way of thanks. The visitors loudly expressed their disappointment at the ugliness of the women and joked about their customers, who must have been blind, or at least desperate, to resort to this human refuse.

Under the rain of prods and curses, one woman still refused to show herself. To avoid the eyes of the others, I kept *my* eyes fixed on her back. She shivered. Her fingers curled tightly around the arms of her chair, as if engaged in an enormous struggle. She gasped for air with great heaves, spreading her chest. The crowd was looking around for a greater challenge and soon fixed its attention on the one person who remained defiant. Desperate to show their superiority, the spectators now directed their most obscene curses at the silent woman, doing their utmost to provoke her.

This display was unbearable. I took Mr Jamieson by the arm. He himself had turned grey with shame and apologised for having brought me to see such a thing. We tried to make our way through the mob to the exit, but the crowd had smelt blood and had no intention of parting to let us through. One of the men even hit my escort and I was forced up against the palisade that separated the prisoners from the visitors. In that instant the solitary woman was hit on the back by a piece of wood that someone had smuggled in. She caught her breath and rose up off her chair with every nerve in her body strung tight. She stood there like that while the whooping subsided into an expectant silence. Everyone was intimidated except one lout who spat a well-aimed gob at her and hit her on the back of the neck. Instead of wiping away the smear, she paused for a few seconds.

I seized this opportunity to squeeze between the spectators and the fence on my way to the exit. In that instant, however, the shrew turned and stormed forward. Like a wild animal, she threw herself against the bars with all her might, so hard the attic droned. Her tormentors recoiled in shock. I did too, but I didn't get far because she stuck her hands through the bars, grabbed me by the arm and tried to pull me towards her, as if I were the prime cause of her suffering. First I was overwhelmed by the filthy stench, as only my veil separated me from her rotten breath, but then I dared to look at her. It was a gruesome sight. Her nose had been eaten down by syphilis, and the rest of her face was so drawn and battered it looked like the devil had danced on it in hobnailed boots. This woman needed to be salved. She was far gone and without a dose of mercury she would soon die.

'Oh God,' I mumbled, 'you poor thing, I am so sorry.'

Sympathy was the last thing she had expected. Her grip weakened. Her face relaxed. She stared at me now with big childish eyes, trying to look through my veil to see whether she knew me. When I attempted to take advantage of this weakness to break free of her grasp, her fury returned. With unexpected strength, she dug her claws deeper into my flesh and pulled me closer. Like a miller who has been caught between the cogs, I was drawn inexorably towards her decaying body. In my terror I screamed for help in my mother tongue. Then I called out the first word that came to mind: of all things, the name I had not spoken aloud since I was a girl. Now, without stopping to think, I repeated it over and over.

★

When did I recognise my Giacomo in that silken French-man? In retrospect I can scarcely believe that it wasn't immediately, the moment we met in the theatre, or maybe even sooner, on hearing his voice under the bridge. In any case, I was sure of it when his wig blew off in the storm by the Amstel. But even after seeing the truth, I still needed time to let myself believe it. It was too shocking. Like someone who has received news of an unexpected death, the situation was clear to me before its significance and consequences had sunk in.

Thinking of my love over the years, I always pictured him as he was the last time I saw him: wandering freely through my mind with big open eyes in an olive face with a downy shadow on his cheeks.

Now, middle-aged features have distorted my image of the youth. His roars of laughter, his playfulness – all the memories I clung to for so many years – with the best will in the world, I couldn't summon them up now.

The man has displaced the boy, and I feel like calling them both to task. In reality, I have no one but myself to blame. I was the one who froze Giacomo in time. Convinced that I would never see him again, I had no reason to adjust his image to the passing years. On the contrary, leaving him unchanged was a solace. The winter that had descended around me was so harsh and merciless that I never expected a thaw.

An external appearance that no longer matches my dreams is one thing. The pale skin, the sharp nose, the full, pouting lips, the hawk-like eyes that follow you as if you were prey, I can get used to all that. I can even step back and see that it still forms an attractive whole. I can see the brazenness as a challenge. And why shouldn't I? It may not be the face I spoke to in my worst moments of darkness, but there is nothing unfriendly about it. It is simply the sum of the elements I neglected to add up.

His inner self is different. Without being aware of it, I had carried its image within me as well. This one had no silhouette or fixed features, and yet I recognised it as my love. Regardless of whether I was imagining his face to go with it, there was always this one certainty dormant within me: that Giacomo's love was greater than mine — bigger, better, nicer. After all, I had felt it myself. I assumed that his understanding of what it meant to love was deeper than mine. More than that, I thought that he *was* love. This may sound vague and woolly-minded to those who don't understand, but people who are like me will know that this awareness was as solid as the ground beneath my feet. It was such an unnamed and indescribable knowledge that it most resembled the quiet certainty of an expectant mother who, feeling the life in her womb, never for a moment needs to ask herself whether she will love the child or whether the child will love her. An emotion like that doesn't reside in the conscious mind. We only become aware of it when we are so unfortunate as to lose it. Our loss forces us to think about what we possessed. Our disappointment reminds us of the expectation we had. It gives it form and allows us to recognise it. Painfully and with gratuitous cruelty, reason overpowers emotion.

That is what happened on the evening I described earlier, when the adult Giacomo killed his younger self before my eyes. It was in front of my own home, when we were saying goodbye in the rain.

'She was a woman,' was all he said.

That was his explanation for not finding me when he returned to Pasiano in the spring.

'She was a woman.'

I closed the door without replying, then stood there listening to his footsteps moving away down the Rusland.

★

For days afterwards I vacillated. At night I couldn't sleep and paced the room. All day long, I was distracted and stayed in bed. Dressing, washing and feeding myself all seemed of secondary importance. I kept the shutters closed.

'*Ma, signora, avanti!*' ventured Danae, when she came by with Giovanna after work to settle up. She did her best to raise my spirits. 'You really must come out dancing with us tomorrow. The city is too sad without you! Just look at yourself, and you're always so careful about your appearance, what's got into you?'

I felt humiliated: more ashamed than sorrowful. How was it possible that I, who had been so hardened by the struggle to survive, could have let myself be overwhelmed by something so obvious: that the years that had made me unrecognisable had done the same to my love? I should have expected it, but I had never stopped to think. With so many uncertainties to overcome every day, my past had been my only security, the only constant I had. It's not possible to contemplate life while living it. Insight is a luxury for those who don't have to worry about the future.

My happy memories were so sparse and so dear to me that I fixed them in my mind, like an artist painting a scene on a canvas. Who stops to think about the drapes being taken down after the sitting, the blinds being drawn and the models going home? Who wants to be reminded that the figures walk away from their positions, curse and stretch, and run to the privy to relieve themselves, anxious to take off their gorgeous clothes and go out boozing? No one questions it: the painter depicts the Last Supper, not the waitress who clears away the dirty dishes afterwards, not the discarded peel or a knocked-over wineglass, not the stains on the tablecloth or the cat that licks the crumbs from the plates.

Giacomo lived on after our separation, of course he did. And thank God. My whole plan was designed to make him forget me and become happy again. It didn't matter that life changed him afterwards, I accepted that, it couldn't have been any other way. But that he should sound so bitter about the betrayal of his first love, and so contemptuous of her fellow females! His remark was self-reproaching, as if the shared past that has completely determined my life was nothing but a lesson every man learns, something he would have seen coming if only he had been a little more experienced . . .

I tried to calm myself. After all, he didn't know my true identity, and if he had, he would not have spoken so harshly. But didn't that just make it worse? Now he voiced his disappointment frankly, giving me the uncensored version, the one he told friends in Venice and drinking companions he encountered at inns on the road, the one that reduced the tragedy of my life to a cheap swindle. In the background I could almost hear him sniggering after reaching the end of the story, laughing the way men laugh about women. Who knows, maybe he had even discussed me with his mistresses to let them know he was up to their tricks.

I blamed myself for his transformation. Would the Giacomo who was in love in Pasiano have changed into the cynical Seingalt if I had listened to my heart at the crossroads of my life? If I had given in to my fierce desire instead of fighting it with reason? If I had dared to show myself to him after my illness, trusting our love enough to subject it to the test, letting life and nature decide instead of sacrificing myself like one of those inane operatic heroines? In that case, I alone would have been disfigured. Now it was both of us.

For three days I wallowed in these lamentations, endlessly running through the most painful sentences in our conversation on the Amstel, especially the ones in which he claimed to have been the constant victim of feminine intrigue. And worst of all: that no one had ever really loved him. I was so fixated on this that it was not until the fourth day that I suddenly remembered a very different part of our conversation. This gave me a very stimulating idea that finally goaded me into action.

I washed and got dressed and went out. At Izaak Duym's, south of the town hall, I bought a fifth of a ream of the best paper and had it trimmed. At home, the sheets lay untouched on the table until evening, but I hovered over them and finally found these words:

Your Lordship, my dear Chevalier,

Not long ago you presented me with a double challenge.

First, to allow you to court me so that I might be able to judge for myself whether you really are that exceptional specimen, a man who does not think solely of himself — something I consider improbable.

Second, to show you a woman who has suffered from having loved you — something you consider impossible.

To dispel my boredom a little, I am prepared to accept your wager. I warn you, however, that I will emerge as the winner whatever the outcome: if you disappoint as a man, you will pay and I will collect my winnings. If you do justice to your self-proclaimed reputation, I will win a number of happy hours in your company. If we part as friends afterwards, as you predict, I will have lost nothing, but if, after spending time together, I am left unhappy, I will be the first exception to your rule. With my sorrow, I will then win the second part of our wager, and you will be obliged to pay me after all.

If you dare to fight this losing battle, I am prepared, for the time being, to fulfil your request and give you the benefit of my love. Until then, yours fondly,

Galathée de Pompignac

The next day I received an invitation from Seingalt to

accompany him to the theatre to see *Harlequin Hulla* and sup with him afterwards. I was somewhat piqued by this, as the comedy in question was only staged on Saturdays and his letter reached me on Thursday. I am not used to being made to wait. Still, I was determined not to mope about it and, since it was Jamieson's regular day, I decided to give him my full attention. I would have been less accommodating had I known that this was the day my American acquaintance had chosen to surprise me with an excursion to the spin-house.

The whore who had seized me by the arm had no intention of letting go. Her nails pressed into my flesh like barbs. Jamieson tried to pull her fingers loose, but in her madness she was stronger. The house father rushed up in answer to my cries for help. He grabbed the harpy by the shoulders and, when this wasn't enough, he put a stick across her throat and pulled back on it with all his might to choke her into letting go. Her grip didn't relax until she had no breath left at all, but even then she had enough life left to claw at me again. She tore several strips off my smock before lashing out one last time and grabbing my veil. She ripped it away, to the general merriment of all present. Then she collapsed, gasping for air. But even on the floor, the madwoman kept staring at me through the bars with wild eyes, while plucking at the threads of my veil.

Unprotected, I stood there in full view of everyone.

Mr Jamieson hadn't seen my scars before. He looked at them without any signs of disgust. For a moment he bowed slightly towards me, as if not quite sure what he was seeing.

'Ah,' he said, without judgement or pity, but almost relieved, as if he had found something he had been searching for. 'Ah, yes.' Then, very briefly, he laid his hand on my cheek. I shivered. His touch felt cool. In all the years, no one had ever touched that spot. He immediately wrapped his

their composure. Some needed to get over the shock, others had to adjust to their feelings of pity, a reaction that has always pained me more. Only then could people look me in the eye, staring hard, as if forcing themselves not to inspect the ruins more closely. People had approached me like that for years. I could hardly remember it being any other way, and it had long since stopped hurting me consciously.

In Holland there was a difference. It is a small country whose people are crowded together. The Dutch are anxious not to be lost in the multitude and try to distinguish themselves from their neighbours. As the inhabitants are so attached to their individuality, differences are not smoothed over out of politeness, but emphasised, especially with foreigners and newcomers. After all, the peculiarities of others can be tremendously helpful in clarifying the image you have of your own perfection. People tolerate difference as long as it is clearly visible. In this sense, my scars were a godsend. People pointed at me and discussed them openly, not just with each other but with me as well. People I did not know at all and had only just met asked innumerable personal questions about the reason for my disfigurement and the sorrow it must have caused me, as if they were trying to chart every nook and cranny of my being different. I assumed that this openness was one of the side effects of the famed tolerance that had attracted the great freethinkers, but it intimidated me, and I found it hard to adjust to.

As a result, it took me some time to realise something the Dutch themselves took for granted: that tolerance is not the same as acceptance. It is actually closer to the opposite: tolerance like this is a clever means of repression. If you accept others as equals, you embrace them unconditionally, now and for ever. But if you let them know that you tolerate them, you suggest in the same breath that they are actually an inconvenience, like a nagging pain or an unpleasant odour you are willing to disregard. Tolerance is cloaked menace:

the mood can change at any moment. Once properly identified, each individual is expected to remain neatly in their allotted position with a clearly legible label, like poison in an apothecary's cabinet. I suspect that this is the real reasoning behind the Dutch mania for identity and individuality. It helps them to slot strange and unfamiliar things into manageable categories, just as they entertain themselves by comparing their public women to horses.

It wasn't easy to make contacts in the new city. People led very private lives. I put this down to the freedom they enjoyed. It's a simple fact that people feel more solidarity when groaning under a strict regime. Amsterdammers are by nature reserved. Even the ones I chatted with on my daily walks never invited me to their homes. In the rest of Europe I had found it easy to live from hand to mouth, but here it was hard to make any headway at all. The city's golden age was over. There were many more hands than jobs. I had hoped to pay my way by teaching, but was unable to obtain a position with any of the wealthy families, not even when I spoke better French than the master of the house himself. I explained that I had grown up on a country estate and had learnt everything there was to know about running a large household at my mother's knee. People replied that Amsterdam's canal houses were modest by comparison and all the positions were taken. I tried in vain to obtain work as a lady's companion or even a lady's maid in a respectable home. Initially I put the rejections down to my appearance, but when I suggested this, people were indignant and insisted that such thoughts were quite foreign to the people of this country. Judging by their shocked reactions, my appearance must have been a recommendation rather than a disadvantage, and it was a terrible shame that the position had always just been filled.

Soon I was forced to give up my comfortable guesthouse

and move in with a widow who rented out a bed at the back of a house on the Oude Waal. I made a futile attempt to secure a position in one of the many shops. A shopkeeper referred me to a workshop that produced cheap imitations of Ghent lace, and I spent one and a half days there before they decided I wasn't suitable: I kept pricking my fingers and bleeding on the strips I was meant to be sewing. At Pasiano I had learnt too few of the skills that were expected of a young woman, and since leaving there, I had neglected them completely. In one of the coach-houses in the Kerkstraat, I found three days' work combing the horses, but after reconsidering, the owner decided that it was an unseemly occupation for a woman. Since I had enjoyed working with my hands, I made some enquiries as to whether there were any estates in the area where I could help the foresters or with the hunt, using the skills I had learnt by watching my father, but for miles around the city there was nothing but water and marsh. I then offered my services as a maid or waitress at the inns. There, at least, people came straight out with it and said that my ugliness would stop prospective guests at the threshold or ruin the appetites of the ones they already had. This was a relief. Honesty is so much gentler than pity. Finally, at a fish market, I found someone who was prepared to put my name on a list for when a large fleet returned to port and women were needed to gut the fish. But the nets stayed empty and life was expensive. I sold Count Antonio's *Dom Bougre* for much less than it was worth. Within six weeks I had exhausted the proceeds and was on my way to a pawnshop. There I left the pendant that my grandfather had made for me, the mirror with the eyes of a saint. I received a paltry amount in return and the date by which I had to redeem it was much too soon. Determined not to lose heart, I kissed my dear memento one last time and swore that I would not lose it.

On the way out someone accosted me. This was unusual

in Dutch cities and I was immediately on my guard, but it was a respectable gentleman. He introduced himself as a surgeon and told me that he was interested in my physiognomy and would like to present me to his students as an example of a smallpox patient. He also offered to pay me for my trouble.

The anatomical theatre was dark when I entered. There was a pungent smell of alcohol and camphor. While removing my outer garments in the adjoining room, I saw frightening shadowy figures – skeletons and stuffed animals – but plucked up my courage and concentrated on the money. It was only when they opened the top shutters in the building, which had once served as a weighing-house, that I saw that I was standing in the middle of an amphitheatre. Sitting around me were some twenty men. They were, I had been assured, trainee surgeons and guild members and highly familiar with the human body. The professor spoke in a reassuring, friendly voice and did nothing without first asking my permission. After describing things in Latin, he even summarised his words in French, solely for my benefit. Once I was used to his pronunciation, I astonished everyone by telling him that I could follow enough of his discourse to understand it without the translation. In essence they were studying the distortion of the skin and the difference between eroded tissues and those where the original pock had healed without bursting. They also looked at my throat and shoulders. Here the professor pointed out places where the pustule had erupted on the inside, spreading poison under the skin. He asked me to copy several movements, which I do in fact always find difficult. He explained this by the presence of hard scar tissue in the muscles, a peculiarity which he promised to demonstrate on the dissecting table later that day. I made a sign of the cross for the poor soul who would take my place and tried to distract myself by studying my surroundings, but everywhere I looked, I saw skeletons, limbs and stillbirths in bottles.

The lesson lasted an hour, after which I was paid and free to go. It remained for me to get dressed in the adjoining room. I was doing just that when the professor came in. I grabbed my skirt to cover my nakedness, but he assured me that in front of a surgeon I had no need to be embarrassed. He had brought a tincture, which he believed might reduce the tension of my scars and make the horny skin more supple again. He meant well and I thanked him. Then he tipped some of the liquid into the palm of his hand and mixed it with oil.

I was not a child and I knew what he wanted. It would be nice to say that I was confused and hesitated, but I don't believe it was like that. I didn't object at all and let him rub it in. When his hands wandered, I made no attempt to stop them. He took me standing. As grateful as a child, he pushed up against me. A satisfied bubble of saliva emerged at the corner of his grinning lips. This brought back involuntary memories from years before of the ruddy face of the Count of Montereale, that dangerous man, innocent and joyful in his pleasure. I let the professor have his way with me, and a lioness, a swan, a crocodile and a snake, all stuffed, witnessed the deed, along with the mounted skin of an anatomised criminal. The showpiece of the room was the skeleton of an elephant, and several of its ribs swayed along to the rhythm of our bodies.

This was the start of my new life in Amsterdam. I left the anatomical theatre as an independent woman with no regrets. An hour later, after retrieving my grandfather's pendant from the pawnshop, I still had enough money left to live for a week. I decided to stop wearing my precious mirror and buried it under my other possessions. I knew that I could not complete the task at hand in front of Lucia's eyes.

★

I'm not saying I didn't shed any tears for the loss of my respectability. Sometimes, when the full weight of reality was bearing down on me, I wept bitterly. At those times I was very aware of the treasure I had surrendered. I knew that it had been my own choice and irreversible, but in my sorrow I still sought ways to escape my fate. I dreamed feverish dreams in which my parents appeared before me so vividly that I thought they were really there, and stretched out my hands as if to touch them. Sometimes I spoke to them, out loud, as if they could hear me. I asked them how they felt and whether they still loved me now that I had disappointed them so deeply. I comforted them too, telling them not to worry, even though they never heard from me. These fits never lasted long. I soon remembered where I was and how far away they were, assuming they were both still alive. The rest of the time I was at peace within myself and felt that the work had changed my status but not my being.

I once had a sailor, a merchant seaman. As soon as his ship docked, he would come to me for a taste of life. One day he told me how once, in heavy weather off the coast of Guinea, he was knocked off the storm jib and into the water. He thrashed around like a man possessed. Terrified, he screamed for help, but no one heard him. Only the sharks. He saw their fins circling around and coming closer and closer, but as soon as they noticed him and turned towards him, his fear disappeared. The idea that he was completely lost and had reached the end of his journey filled him from one moment to the next with a profound peace, a satisfaction he had never known before. He stopped fighting and gave himself over to the waves in a way a man, he said, can normally only give himself over to a woman's bosom. In a state of bliss. At that moment a boat appeared, disturbing everything. His shipmates beat off the sharks' attack. When they threw the drowning man a line, he was almost disappointed. He had passed a point and no longer wanted to return. Only after he passed out did they succeed in dragging him into the boat.

I have known that kind of peace, a grace found only in the deepest hopelessness. To those who have not experienced it, it can only remain a mystery. As long as life is presenting solutions, our brains work at full speed. We feel responsible for our own fate and want the best outcome, but are terrified of making the wrong decision. More than the possible result, it is choice itself that causes us to despair. Doubt makes us restless. It is only in extreme situations – when we feel that our fate has been decided and there is nothing we can do about it – that we stop thinking. Finally, we dare to trust our intuition. There is no time left to hesitate. We surrender to our first impulse and, by doing so, find peace. By doing so, we survive.

That, at least, is how I came through the deepest humiliations. Shame was embedded in my flesh like a harpoon. As long as I left it alone, it was relatively painless, but whenever I tried to pull it out, it cut deeper. Over the last few years, I have made many decisions with this knowledge in the back of my mind. After all, this wasn't the first time I had been forced to accept my life's branching off from the route I had plotted in my dreams.

I learnt from my sailor in that sense as well. As a young man he had hoped to become a captain and set his own course, but he had soon realised that it would never happen. His work was heavy. It broke his back and cut his hands. It made him ill and dirty and homesick. That didn't mean that he derived no satisfaction from his adventures. After each voyage, he signed up again.

I returned to the anatomical theatre several times, but the professor lost interest. On my final visits, for the same fee, I let him talk me into standing beside the dissecting table as a model. 'If Signora Morandi can bear it,' I thought, 'so can I.'

During the lesson I demonstrated the function of muscles in the living body while the professor cut them out of a cadaver and held them up for his students. Once he pressed the dead tissue against my bare back to show how short a particular muscle was in rest and how far it stretched from its point of attachment. I didn't flinch, and resolved that I would never go back there again.

After this I went to great lengths to support myself in my little room, but soon aroused the suspicions of the widow I was lodging with. She had banned relations with men under her roof and threw me out despite my arrears. My decline was rapid. I went from a bed to straw, and from straw to the floor.

I am not relating all this because I think it says anything about my character. Better women have gone down this same path, along with worse. The story serves as a sketch of the times and the conditions I had to survive in. They were hard years. Holland's prosperity was fading and its dominion over the seas had passed to England. In Amsterdam there were thousands of women like me.

My career as a streetwalker was brief, and I never frequented the Kalverstraat, where the twopenny whores plied their trade. Late in the afternoon, I would walk past the carpenters' yards to the Plantation and promenade there at my leisure. I solicited my customers with a glance and settled the transaction between the bushes or, in winter, in the shelter of the orangery. It was customary to remain silent. This was crucial. It allowed some kind of illusion to be maintained, so that the client could fantasise that it was a real amourette. It was also possible to slip into one of the inns, but they had a bad name. Many men were afraid to be seen in them, and I preferred the outdoors. Even when the customers were unpleasant, I found a certain consolation in the surroundings. Subdued green foliage around my head or sharp twigs scratching my skin. Rustling branches moving in time to our play. The elastic pressure of a thin trunk against my back. Bark under my fingers. The warm, heady smells of moss, wood and resin rising on a summer's evening as the cool night air drew the dew up out of the ground. There were so many things to distract me from what was really happening. More than anything else, I remember my feet sinking slowly under the weight, deeper and deeper into the soil.

Sometimes I was surprised that these things didn't repulse me as they should. It's tempting to say that the vegetation took me back to my happiest years at Pasiano, where I was surrounded by nature. There I chose my playmates from the animals and rode the horses the way they walked the fields. As a child I was unafraid and unjudged. Nothing limited my happiness, because at Pasiano there were no dangers. That couldn't be said of the Amsterdam Plantation. In the brief period I worked it, three bodies were discovered among the seedlings. Women who had had their throats cut after being used. The comparison with Pasiano does not hold. It's just that the Plantation's charms helped me to bear the grossness of the work. Despite the discomforts, I was never able to shut out reality as fully as I could when working in the open air. Later, turning tricks in spill-houses or back rooms, there was no escaping the oppressive bleakness. In natural surroundings there was always a sense of freedom and the feeling that escape was possible. Among nettles and with the scent of roses in the air, my situation was so outlandish that it seemed almost abstract; participating in it, I did not feel that it was really me. The only similarity with Pasiano: I remember no limits.

Soon, however, I was press-ganged by a bully, one of the disreputable characters who demand money for protection, mainly from themselves. He found a place for me in a whorehouse in the shadow of the Herring Packer's Tower, close to the port. The people who came there were the dregs of the dregs, as it was frequented mainly by the crews of East Indiamen. Every day ships moored whose men had not seen a woman in months. They inundated the city by the thousand with money in their pockets and mad with lust. They were like a tribe of savages, and if we hadn't been there to let them blow off steam, they might have raped all of the city's daughters and mothers. The work was hard and filthy. Most of them were unwashed and unshaven. Even worse: they came up with the most bizarre fantasies, grotesque fancies that had preyed on their lonely minds during the long voyage and which they now wanted to see fulfilled. Often I ended up in the middle of a tangle of bodies in positions you would sooner expect from a condemned man who has been stretched over a wheel by the sheriff. Like the rest of them, these demanding clients had full purses, and the bullies and the madam made sure we emptied them as soon as possible. Refusal was not an option. Deception was. I developed my skills. First I plied my customers with drink and then, if they were still capable, I would attempt to simulate the acts they demanded. Often I succeeded. Oafs like these were usually far gone and relatively inexperienced at anything beyond handwork. (It was here, by the way, that I one day recognised the 'Count of Saint Germain'. The former companion of Jesus Christ had been forced to flee Paris and intended to start a porcelain factory in Weesp, a plan that he was no doubt forced to reconsider once I had thoroughly fleeced him.)

I remained in this position long enough to pay off my bully. Afterwards the spill-houses, where I worked for myself, came as a relief. Spill-house girls were free to choose and never had to do anything against their wishes. With my looks, I obviously couldn't attract the best customers, but in these establishments even the less choosy men were generally God-fearing citizens. Most of them bought their love not of necessity, but as a luxury, a refinement that made them appreciate us all the more. And a woman who is more appreciated begins to value herself more highly. I started to dress more smartly and took better care of myself. I ate better and grew rounder and fuller, attracting wealthier clients as a result. Meanwhile I perfected my skills. I derived quite a few of my tricks, by the way, from the story of Dom Bougre, the gatekeeper of Chartreux, which I had carried around with me for so long that I knew the prints like the back of my hand. More and more I was able to pleasure men without having to resort to real intercourse, so that they went home contented and I was left unsullied.

In these better houses, they also peddled 'condums'. These sheaths were a medical invention best known among surgeons, and until then I had only seen one in the dissecting theatre with the professor. Made from the intestines of cats or calves, they provided protection against infection. The madam insisted on their use. Besides guaranteeing her girls' health, they also stopped them from getting pregnant and too big to work. Many men, however, were reluctant to wear them. Rather than realising that a woman who insisted on one of these preservatives must be more hygienic than the rest, they believed that she must want it because she was already infected. This is typical male logic. That was why it was important to encourage the gentleman first and then slip on the sheath at the point where he would have put on anything, even a cap and bells, if it let him carry on without interruption.

One day when I was leaving one of these houses, a gentleman approached me. I had never seen him before. He wasn't a customer. My suspicions were aroused, but he assured me that he only wanted to have a drink together. We went to the coffee house next to the Gentlemen's Guest-house, a respectable establishment and completely above-board, and there we spent two very pleasant hours. He was erudite and spoke to me about books and philosophy, things I had been unable to share with anyone in Amsterdam, simply because the people I associated with were completely ignorant of them. In mid-conversation he stood up, made his apologies and asked if he might meet me again sometime. He paid me for my time but disappeared without obliging me with his name or address, something I found unexpectedly disappointing.

Two weeks later, he was there again, this time early in the evening, just as I was about to enter the house. He asked me whether I would care to dine with him. I refused as I needed to earn my money, but he promised to make it worth my while. The meal was exquisite and again our conversation sparkled. At the end of the evening, shy and almost embarrassed, he handed me an envelope. I opened it. It contained a charming tract he had described during our previous encounter. The pamphlet discoursed upon the garden of the imagination, and was illustrated with plates showing the garden in full blossom and choked by weeds. He had acquired it especially for me. I was touched. I can't explain why, but tears rushed to my eyes. It had been a long time. It was absurd to think that I had come through so many horrors in this city dry-eyed only to be broken by this small kindness. I was afraid that he would misinterpret my behaviour, but couldn't control myself.

'When someone touches us,' he said, 'we realise how alone we are.' He left me with the reimbursement he had promised and a note with his name, Texeira, and an address on the Nieuwe Herengracht.

'If you care to go there, they will be glad to receive you.'

At the house in question, a caretaker showed me to a small

second-floor flat that had been prepared for me. I moved in early the next day. My benefactor visited me there several times a week, supporting me completely in return. By letting him keep me, I turned my back on my old life, and was able to start putting a little money aside as well. I felt a cautious hope that my life might have taken a turn for the better. The evenings I spent with Texeira had none of the lustre I had known in Bologna or Vincennes, but our conversations revived my spirits and aroused my curiosity, which had lulled without my realising it.

I remember how before, during my illness, my feverish body had switched off all functions that were not essential to my short-term survival. It was only when I began to recover that I realised how lifelessly I had lain there. My mind must have felt a similar threat during my whoring and, without my noticing, shut itself off from verve and *esprit*. Now Texeira's humour and intelligence prodded these traits to wake them from their hibernation. Drowsily, ideas and beliefs emerged from their hiding place. They stretched and gazed around in astonishment at the new life that seemed to have begun. I looked forward to Texeira's visits and enjoyed catching up on lost time.

This happiness was brief.

There was a young girl living in the flat below mine. She was Danae, and this was how I met her. She was being kept by a friend of Texeira's. We were on friendly terms but led separate lives. One evening we decided to go out together, the four of us, but it was not a success. The girl was fearful. She didn't want to stay anywhere long. During dinner she was nervous and kept looking around, and whenever people came in she jumped. The next day I spoke to her about it. I told her how carefree my new life was and asked if anything was wrong with hers.

'It's nothing,' she replied. 'My maintainer is good to me. Really, there's not a kinder soul in the world, it's just . . .

Well, of course, it's the same as Mr Texeira.' As if she had clarified everything, she changed the subject so casually that I decided that I was at fault for not understanding her. I let her finish what she was saying, but before going upstairs I plucked up my courage and asked what she had actually been referring to. She looked at me with surprise.

'You know,' she said, 'a Jew's a Jew.'

Only three days later – I had just fallen asleep with my head on Texeira's chest after love – constables smashed in the door with an axe. They pulled us out of bed, manacled us roughly, pushed us downstairs and loaded us onto a wagon. Danae and her lover were already lying there. Bystanders spat and jeered at us as if we were Gypsies. The constables carted us off to prison, where we had to wait ten days for trial with nothing to wear except the sheets we had hurriedly torn from the bed.

It turned out that the law in Amsterdam strictly forbids sexual relations between Jews and Christians. Besides the freedom to live there and practise their religion, Jews are not allowed any privileges at all, and since they are often wealthy and can afford stiff fines, they are persecuted fanatically. Until Danae told me this, I had no idea, and even then I could scarcely believe it. It was true that you never saw them in brothels, but it hadn't occurred to me that this was because of any special rules. On the contrary, I had been told that Holland had always been very hospitable to the Jews, and I couldn't understand why people nowadays agitate so fiercely against relations with this people. I wonder whether Messieurs Voltaire and Descartes were aware of this when they praised Dutch liberty.

I spent two whole years in the spin-house. The discipline was harsh. The atmosphere among the women, hard. In the cells you had to fight for everything: a pallet, a chunk of bread, a chemise, a needle, sometimes even the right to catch a breath of fresh air at an open window. Disagreements were fought out with bare hands, but also with combs and scissors. This was still better than what happened in the attic, where we were on constant display the whole day long. The behaviour of the paying visitors taught me more about the human soul than I wanted to know. Suffice to say that any physical abnormality fed their bloodlust. In all those years, there was *one* woman who regularly took my side. She was a gruff character who was serving a long sentence for selling souls. In other words, she had practised the trade of getting seamen into debt and forcing them to sign a note promising to reship. That made her the owner of their lives, which she resold to the East India Company or some other shipping firm. She was used to dealing with sailors, and when the people who came to view us went too far, she would stick up for me like a man. Although she was usually surly and sullen about her fate, she was the only prisoner who stood up and embraced me when I was finally released.

I hadn't seen her since and had no idea she was so ill. When she grabbed me after I had returned to the spin-house as a spectator with Mr Jamieson, I hardly recognised her, her face was so chancrous.

Texeira had bought himself out of the rasp-house. He had moved to The Hague and was so ashamed of the suffering he had caused me that he couldn't face me. That was fine by me, because I was furious and overflowing with the filthiest recriminations. He did offer to support me with an allowance I was in no position to refuse. I used it to rent a room on the Rusland and a small flat for Danae, whose friend had showed less sense of responsibility. She resumed her former work and paid for her lodgings by handing over a percentage of her takings. Later, she took in a friend of hers under the same conditions, Giovanna, who came from Parma as well and attracted customers by claiming to be the daughter of a Venetian nobleman, a lie that could only fool a blind man with no sense of smell.

For myself, I was unable to go back to that existence. I needed time to recover. Just leaving the house was difficult enough. I could no longer appreciate the openness of the Dutch. The looks people gave me hurt me more than they had before. When someone greeted me, as always, by looking at my scars first and then at me, I would flinch, as if the chorus of abuse I knew from the spin-house was about to erupt over me again. The friendliness with which people then put aside their fright and pity now stung me, and the pain made me disagreeable. No matter how kind they were, my tongue was sharp and unforgiving. When I saw my victims blanch before me, I was disgusted with myself and the kind of woman I had become. For so many years, I had succeeded in keeping my disfigurement on the outside, but now, thanks to my embitterment, it had finally turned inward. I was afraid for my soul and the only salvation I could see was to hide the stain that made me different, just as I had once done in Venice. Without realising that doing so would turn my weakness into my greatest strength, I decided to wear a veil.

This is my life. It happened this way.

However, rather than dwelling in this past, I am attached to the present. Of course, I hesitated before describing these sordid events. I would have preferred to make myself more beautiful or, better still, to have kept silent. Raking over my past isn't easy. It's a task I would never have begun without a clear goal in sight: engendering understanding for the considerations and decision I am about to relate. To do that I need to tell the whole truth, even at the cost of squandering

3

Giacomo is sitting beside me in the Amsterdam Theatre.

It seems that fate delights, an actress on the stage declaims, *in separating me from those who love me.*

He couldn't be closer. The auditorium is full. We are squeezed in together. When his chest expands, our sides touch. For minutes at a time we breathe to the same rhythm, like people who have been together their whole life. As if I crept into his bed one morning in Pasiano and never left it again.

Then he escapes me by bursting out laughing. One of the farce's jokes has the audience in stitches. I haven't been listening. He turns toward me, wanting to share the fun. I laugh heartily, not knowing why. It disrupts our rhythm. The laughter presses all the air out of his lungs. His shoulders shake. He catches his breath with a few quick gasps. He lets out one last chuckle, and then we come back together. In and out. His ribs against my side. Out. In. I think I can even feel his heartbeat now, or is it my own?

Where were you born, Fatima? asks the actress, her eyes big with surprise. *Crying about losing a man! Is that the fashion in these parts?*

All day I have been nervous, regretting my recklessness and wishing that I had never sent Giacomo my brazen challenge. A wager with love as the stakes! How could I have thought that I could keep up a bluff like that in his presence? My recent excursion to the spin-house has wrecked me. It brought my past back to life, while my future seems murkier than ever. The last thing I need now is to let myself get even more confused. God knows what kind of adventures I have brought down on myself with that grand bet of mine because, to be frank, I have no plan at all.

Less than an hour before leaving home, I was considering cancelling the whole thing. I had laced myself into my best dress and was putting on a new veil of fine Indian gossamer, when suddenly I panicked. At the last minute, I wanted to flee from this ordeal, just as I had tried to escape the woman who sold souls. I plucked up my courage and decided to consider the situation reasonably. What did I want? What could I do? I saw four possibilities.

(1) Most of all, I would like to erase the lost years and pick up from where I – compelled by circumstance – broke things off. This longing is hopeless. My disappearance changed him for ever; I have been changed by life. The Lucia and Giacomo from Pasiano no longer exist. They have both murdered the innocents they were and adopted new names.

(2) More realistic: I could take things as they are. Lay my cards on the table, telling him what *I* know but he cannot suspect. This course would compel me to reveal my true identity to my former love and allow me to explain what I hoped to achieve through my 'betrayal' and how deeply sorry I am that my ploy miscarried. But would this change him? Wouldn't the truth come too late for that? Monsieur is

so comfortably ensconced in his convictions. He has built his merry little life upon those foundations. Would he be willing and able at this late stage to do justice to Lucia, to me, by changing his opinion of her? In the most extreme case, I would be forced to show him the reason for my departure, the very thing I had hoped to spare him: my face. I could raise my veil and throw myself at his feet. This would leave two possibilities: he might loathe me, which would mean my death; or he would understand everything, overcome his aversion and be overwhelmed by pity. The latter, for me, would be worse than dying.

(3) Remain silent and leave him in the delusion that Galathée de Pompignac has nothing to do with his Lucia. In this case we would play the game of love a second time as equals. Adults now and feeling each other out. I could discover his true character, studying him to my heart's content and plumbing his depths. Yes, he might even fall in love with me again, with the woman I am now. And I could fall in love with him. But then? Where would we go from there? Afterwards I would never be able to reveal my true identity to him. After all, he could never forgive such deceit. Once more I would need to disappear, and once more he would feel betrayed. In his thoughts, I would always be Galathée de Pompignac, the latest in a long line of treacherous women, and his contempt for Lucia would remain unchanged.

(4) Flee then after all? Let him go to the theatre and not join him. He would find this so insulting that he would refuse to see me again. He would never discover my true identity. His image of Lucia would not alter. Everything would stay the same. Holding his next conquest in his arms, he would tell her about the first love who made such a fool of him, and together the brand-new turtle doves would scoff at the wiles of an Italian chambermaid.

I sat paralysed before the mirror in my best clothes. It was time to leave for my assignation, but between all the losses I foresaw from this enterprise I could not detect the slightest gain. Unless, of course, it was the few hours I might spend in Giacomo's proximity. I cursed the letter in which I had boasted that I must emerge victorious from this affair; the opposite seemed closer to the truth. Only magic could save me now.

In that instant I remembered how Zélide had advised me not to think about important decisions: when in doubt, withdraw in silence, close your eyes and take a few deep breaths. Then do the first thing that comes to you. 'Reason,' she said, 'offers us many possibilities. Intuition infallibly chooses the best.'

I closed my eyes.

People are only capable of wanting one thing at a time.

Having Giacomo next to me and concentrating on the performance at the same time really is asking too much. We keep our eyes on the stage, but I virtually ignore the play. I delight in sitting silently beside him, so naturally. Now his breathing quickens. His upper body tenses. He moves slightly and leans towards me. He puts an arm over the back of my seat to get closer. Cautiously he pulls me towards him.

'Do you see now,' he whispers, 'what kind of misunderstandings something like that can lead to?'

I purr my assent, as mysterious and omniscient as a sphinx, but I don't have a clue what he's referring to. For a second the tip of his nose brushes my ear lobe. I need to concentrate on the farce. Later, he will want to discuss it. Thank God, he sits up straight again and doesn't ask any more questions.

A veiled woman is standing on the boards.

There is some confusion about her identity.

Out of the corner of my eye, I look at Giacomo. He knew this piece and obviously chose it for a reason.

It is set in Turkey in the palace of the mufti, who has fallen in love again with the woman he once repudiated.

My heartbeat picks up. With quick, shallow breaths, my ribs leave the calm swelling and subsiding of Giacomo's behind them.

According to the law of Muhammad, however, the mufti cannot take her back until she has been married to another. The imam thinks of a solution and engages an Italian, Harlequin, to marry Zaida and repudiate her the same night without laying a finger on her, after which the mufti will be free to make her his wife again. By chance, however, this Harlequin happens to be the stranger who saved Zaida from drowning – the man she really loves. The unhappy couple spend their wedding night in the same room without realising their true identities. Fully dressed, they can't wait for morning to come. With Zaida veiled and Harlequin in darkness, they don't even realise how close their happiness has come.

The audience has stopped laughing and is holding its breath.

It all ends with a ballet and a Turkish woman who sings:

> *Oh lovers, listen and take heart,*
> *There is no foe you cannot beat,*
> *Miraculous love will take your part,*
> *And conjure triumph from defeat.*

'I am a disciple of the moment,' declares Giacomo.

We are sitting in a *chambre separée* at the City Inn. The door and walls of the small, octagonal room are hidden behind curtains of cobalt-blue moquette. A soft divan covered with orange cushions is shamelessly enticing in the semi-darkness. Although I keep it to myself, I am no stranger to this room. The last time I supped here with a gentleman, I myself turned out to be dessert.

Giacomo laughs again at the mufti's foolishness in going to such lengths to possess a woman.

'Contracts binding two people would be a fine idea if life were immutable. But it's constantly taking us by surprise. "Improvise," it calls out to us, "anticipate, vary!" One must be prepared at all times to change course, don't you think? Eternal faithfulness is a religion for fools or nuns who get themselves walled into their cells.'

Someone knocks on the door. The waiter comes in. Giacomo leans back and languidly gives his order. He does not bother to pretend that he is unfamiliar with this kind of rendezvous. Strangely, his attitude nettles me. I was so much happier to have him silent beside me than holding forth across from me. The way he plays the man of the world annoys me. Or perhaps I dislike his being a man of the world. Belonging to the world when he could have been mine. The world took him away from me. Is it fair to hold that against him?

'And yet even you once hoped to marry,' I say as soon as we are alone again.

'Me?' He is genuinely astonished. 'When might that have been?'

I feel a sudden urge to hit him, but impress upon myself the need to persist in being the woman he takes me for.

'It was undoubtedly a moment of indescribable weakness,' I counter, 'but still . . . You told me about it yourself. Your very first girl . . . somewhere outside Venice? Yes, more to the point, you were disappointed when the festivities were cancelled.'

'Oh, that. I was a child.'

'She was a hard lesson, but you evidently learnt from it.'

'I learnt not to let anyone else capture my heart.'

'Do you mean to say the ungrateful wench is still holding it hostage?'

'No one has ever loved me more than she did. That did not stop her from betraying me without hesitation or regret.'

'You cannot possibly know that.'

'That's true. And until the day I understand why my faithfulness deserved no better, I refuse to bind myself to anyone for life.'

'So you haven't been faithful to anyone since then?'

'On the contrary, I have always been faithful, without exception, to every love anew.'

'But never for life . . .'

'You seem so fond of this hobby-horse, madame, that I am beginning to worry that I may have been mistaken in you. From your letter, I concluded that your challenge was an invitation for me to entertain you, but now you sound like one of those women whose greatest wish is to be chained up once and for all.'

'Most definitely not, monsieur.' I now have his tone down pat, that gently mocking disdain. 'What does marriage do besides turning talented men into husbands and making brilliant women their slaves?'

A guinea hen is brought in. The head waiter sharpens his knives, plants them in the flesh and debones the bird with a few deep slashes.

'My dear chevalier, my only concern is winning my wager. To that end I surely need to draw up an inventory of your thoughts on love and the ways you have made love to date?'

'They are no different to the way I plan to make it again,' he ventured, 'and as soon as possible. Given the opportunity I will gladly provide you with all necessary pointers and the proofs you require. Afterwards you can elaborate and classify them to your heart's content.'

'Are you always in such a rush?'

'I do not have much time left in this city. At the start of next year I am expected in Paris to report to the government on the progress I have made here.' There is a brazen glint in his eye. 'I trust that I will be able to report success on all fronts.'

I refuse to concede the point and tease him a little more.

'If you have never disappointed anyone, as you claim, surely it can only mean that you never aroused high expectations in the ladies concerned.'

He responds with a self-confident chuckle.

'Monsieur, if none of your lady friends have lamented your departure from their lives, I can only envisage two possible causes: your performance in their arms was so abominable that they were only too glad to forgo any further engagements . . .'

'Guess again,' he says, unfazed.

'. . . or else you were always unambiguous towards them and clear about your desires from the very beginning.'

'Never any less clear than you, in your letter to me. Although I must say that I generally manage to frame the conditions less severely. But, of course, *I* need to win over women, and sweet talk happens to make them more susceptible. *You* only need to convince a man, a creature that would come running if you whistled in the street.'

'There is no justice in the world,' I laugh. 'You must go to great lengths to obtain something you want immediately, while we can get the thing we least desire anywhere with no questions asked.'

'You do your sisters an injustice. I have known countless women who were so hungry for love that a man could scarcely keep up with them.'

'In your hurry, you probably never had time to notice that a woman derives her pleasure from the game, whereas the man only wants to push on to victory.'

'Not at all. I am just as satisfied mapping out my strategy as I am hauling in the loot.'

'Then we are well matched,' I say, clinking glasses. '*Santé!*'

★

During the meal, he tells me about some of his wildest adventures. More than the content, I am struck by his tone. It is invariably formal, as if we are conversing in a salon where the guests are constantly trying to outdo each other with witticisms. I don't want it to be like that, and I try to remember how we used to sound in the days when I would creep onto his bed early in the morning with herbs I had picked for his tea and he would tell me off because the dirt from the roots fell onto his sheets.

He notices that I am only half listening, and asks about me and my life. He undoubtedly knows from experience that this kind of interest works with women. I tell him a few things that he cannot possibly connect with Pasiano. I have adjusted my tone. Instead of trying to make my words sparkle, I talk straight from my heart. This brings us closer together, but it also encourages him to be more personal.

'Haven't you ever promised your heart to someone?'

'Of course,' I reply. 'Like you, I gave it away while I was still very young, that very first time.'

'And does it still belong to that lucky fellow?'

We are midway through the second course, a veal pastry, and I am starting to question my ability to maintain the deception until the end.

'We lost track of each other.'

'Carelessness like that is proof enough. I take it that you agree with me that one must sometimes adjust one's expectations regarding faithfulness.'

'In practice, yes. Life goes on. In theory, I still cherish the innocence of that first promise, more than life itself. More than all the things I have been told or seen proven since. In my darkest moments, it comforts me to know that once there was something that was indisputably genuine.'

'But even that most genuine of promises, you couldn't keep.'

'So what!' My voice breaks. I pretend that I am choking

and drink a few mouthfuls. Suddenly I am afraid that I will slip into the familiar gestures that betrayed me to his brother in Venice. But Francesco was more attentive than Giacomo, more sensitive perhaps as well. What's more, so many years have passed. They have taken their toll. My voice is deeper, my shoulders lower, my figure fuller than it used to be. No, as long as I keep wearing my veil, I don't need to worry about being exposed. I continue in a calmer voice, 'It is the only constant I have, you see: my faith that we both meant what we said.'

'Then you have known more happiness than I.'

'How could we have been anything but genuine in our innocence?'

My question is so direct and urgent that he doesn't dare reply. I am finding it increasingly difficult now to keep up the pretence of being a stranger to him. He tops up my glass and his own, and cuts the pastry on his plate, deep in thought.

'I don't believe I was ever innocent. I know that in my youth I upheld a number of values which were dragged down in time by life.'

'I'm so sorry.'

'Why?' he sneered. 'It's hardly your fault.'

I have to bite my lip to control myself. He can't possibly see it, but he guesses.

'It's no great drama, Gala.'

That name. It is the first time he has addressed me with this name. It sounds sweet on his lips. Still, I would have rather heard the other one.

'Surely you don't cherish the same longings you had as a girl?' Briefly he lays his hand on mine. 'Growing up means facing reality.'

I would like to provide him with the repartee he expects, but I can't. It's too much for me. Too many things are rushing in on me. I feel inadequate. After all I have been through, have I really made so little progress? Is the desire I feel tonight really so different from what I felt then? I am jealous as well. Because he seems to have come further than me. When I left Pasiano to go off into the world, I thought I was leaving him behind. Now it seems that I was the one who was left behind.

'When Marco Polo returned from the Great Khan he told of holy men who had so much respect for life that they used faggots to sweep the ground before their feet. They wanted to be absolutely certain that they wouldn't stand on any living creatures. Only then would they take a step forward. They died without harming so much as an insect, but they never got very far from home.'

'Maybe they were already where they wanted to be,' I said.

'High standards are a wonderful starting point. When we are young they protect us from the follies of youth. People who cling to them afterwards, inhibit their development. We can't possibly live up to them and live life at the same time.'

'So you trample all over them.'

'They fall by the wayside. That's unavoidable. They die one after the other, like brave soldiers. If you don't like it, you're better off hiding in a cloister. There you won't hurt anyone and no one will hurt you and you can believe the things your parents told you until the end of your days.'

'You are so disillusioned!'

'Not at all. If you keep your eyes on reality you cannot become disillusioned.'

'So now you call the values you had as a young man illusions?' I exclaim, suddenly fierce. 'And what do you call the idiots who let you take them in, the ones who were foolish enough to believe you heart and soul?' It sounds indignant. I'm slipping out of my role. He looks at me quietly, as if listening to the echo of my anger and trying to locate its source.

'Saying goodbye to illusions is always heartbreaking,' he says sympathetically, 'but I have always felt a great beauty in that sorrow.'

'Speak clearly!'

'We cry when someone we love dies, but at the same time we realise more keenly than ever that we are still alive. We resolve that henceforth we will experience what we have left of this miracle even more intensely. The truth is a hard taskmaster that punishes every slip of attention. It shows up our ideals the same way. We mourn this loss and cling all the more tightly to what we have left.'

'And that is?'

'Not as lofty, but more reliable. Less unrealistic, more reasonable. We leave our state of nature further and further behind and develop from emotional creatures into rational beings. This is the beauty I feel in the loss of illusion: the pain proves that we have taken another step on the path of reason.'

'And the insect underfoot, that knows nothing higher than its nature?'

Giacomo shrugs.

'Alas!' He smacks his hands together, as if crushing the little creature before my eyes. The unexpected clap interrupts my thoughts so suddenly that I let out a cry of fright.

'You know exactly what I mean, don't you? Life has shaped you in the same way, *chère* Galathée. Not gently moulding, but with the hard blows of a sharp chisel. Otherwise your reaction would not be this intense.'

I shiver. Taking that as a sign, he stands up and puts an arm around me. I let him have his way.

Some of the candles have burnt down, the room is almost dark. I force myself to consciously feel each caress, but only partly succeed. Over the years I have imagined this moment in hundreds of different ways, from rough to solemn. Now that it is actually happening, the situation seems less real than my dreams. I cannot surrender to it. His lips on my throat. I groan softly the way I do, dutifully, but I don't feel him, I don't feel that now it is *him*, that it's me. The game we have been playing with our identities this evening has led my body astray. Giacomo notices and hesitates for a moment before gently continuing. He runs his nails down my back. 'This is *him*,' I tell myself, 'his hand, his body. Think about it, this is the moment that was always missing from your life! You had abandoned all hope of it years ago and now . . .' And now? I put his hands on my breasts. I raise my veil slightly to let him kiss me. His lips brush mine. I feel his breath on my throat.

Then he stops.

'I'm sorry.' He sits up straight. 'This is unforgivable, I know, but I can't do it. It's impossible. Not tonight. Forgive me, for God's sake.'

Maintaining as much dignity as possible, I scramble up. I straighten my garments and mumble something frivolous. It has the wrong effect. He hides his face in his hands. He gasps for breath. Now I am the one to lay my arm around his shoulders, but he shrugs me off and stands up as if to escape me.

I think . . . I don't know what I think. I think all kinds of things at once. That he has discovered my identity after all. That he has guessed at my disfigurement. That I don't match up to his other mistresses. Perhaps, God forbid, he has suddenly been taken ill. Maybe I've exposed myself like a whore and frightened him off.

His face in the light of the last candle. He bends forward with one hand on the table. With the other he pours a glass of wine, then gulps it down as if he needs to recover from something. I go over to him, take his hand and stroke it, as if consoling a child that's fallen over.

'Our conversation,' he says eventually. 'It keeps running through my mind. The way you made me think about things.'

I apologise, although I am unsure what exactly I am apologising for.

'Forcing my mind back to things, to a time . . . A time I thought I had left behind.' His breathing is uneven, he slumps down on a chair. He shakes his head ruefully. 'It shouldn't be like this. You and I. It's not fair. I want to be there completely for you. Body and soul. Being elsewhere with my thoughts is not right. Even if it's with a ghost from the past.'

I stiffen. 'He knows everything!' I think, but tell myself that's impossible.

'On another occasion, assuming I am granted another chance, Galathée, because I certainly haven't earned it, I will more than make it up to you, I promise,' he says remorsefully. 'But tonight? No.'

'For heaven's sake, what's wrong with you?' I take his face in my hands.

'Our wager. My thoughts. They're with the past. You've set me doubting. It's the things you ask. The things you suggest.' He turns away again, as if trying to pluck up courage for what comes next. 'What if I really have hurt someone?'

'Then it wouldn't have been deliberate,' I say soothingly.

'I swear it. It's just . . . imagine it did happen once or, God forbid, more than once, then . . .'

'Then?'

This big strong man, he looks like he's about to cry. A tear wells up, glinting in the candlelight.

'Who can assure me I won't do it again?'

Neither of us says another word. I know what I have to do. I stand before him and undress. I take off everything except my veil. That's how I dry his tears. I unbutton him, his trouser flaps, behind which I find a manhood not nearly as crestfallen as his words. I take hold of him and kiss Giacomo until nature snatches the initiative out of my hands.

He throws himself on me, biting, growling. We roll over the floor like puppies. I let him press me down, knowing I will rise up all the more powerfully after. He does the same. We leave no time to stop and think. The wrestling keeps our lust alert. Soon my lover has to grab the legs of the divan to save himself from grazing his back on the floorboards. I mount him and pace myself, galloping and trotting in turn. His eyes roll back with pleasure. His objections are forgotten. For a moment I feel pride at being the one who has achieved this. Then the truth hits me.

Suddenly, in the middle of all this, I see through him. A man so seasoned in love knows every strategy. He has learnt to think like the women he wants to conquer. This knowledge is his secret weapon. Isn't it obvious that he has just used it against me? To fix my attention on the task at hand. How could a man win a woman more completely than by revealing unexpected sensitivity? Giacomo is so sophisticated at this game that he knows that pity can make a woman's fire rage. Of course he does. By feigning doubt, he let vulnerability shine through his formal conversation. Isn't it obvious that his sudden anxiety was just a pretence to gain my sympathy, a device to arouse me by melting my heart, hoping that I would try to comfort him by taking more initiative, just as I, fool that I am, am now doing?

I see it all in a flash. But I block out the thought, just as I have learnt to close my eyes to anything I don't want to see. It is too late to turn the tide of lust. Under my thighs I feel his stomach muscles contract. I feel his life in mine. I concentrate completely on this pleasure and, with unfeigned excitement, ride him out.

4

I was seeking distance. When I lowered a veil in front of the world soon after being released from the spin-house, it was so I could withdraw. The first one I bought was made of a fabric from Gaza. The mesh was not especially fine, but the cloth was dotted with skilfully embroidered ladybirds that blurred the view in, but let me look out unimpeded. In Venice people go out in all kinds of masks, but in Amsterdam it was an unusual sight. Noble ladies occasionally wore veils, but only at the theatre or a ball. On the street you might see a masked person in a carriage, but never simply walking by a canal.

It took great courage for me to go out like that. At home in front of the mirror, I tried on the veil at least five or six times. I procrastinated more than I had the first time I walked the street. I was surprised that it was easier for me to go out as a whore than a lady. But that's the way of it: it takes more courage to cover yourself than it does to lay yourself bare.

I went out first at twilight, resolved to stick to the shadows and stay close to home. I was immediately noticed. That was nothing new. I always stood out. My new outfit was as conspicuous as my scars, but the attention I attracted was different. There was no repulsion and no sign of its opposite, pity, either. More people stared, but it affected me less. They looked up with puzzled expressions and wondered why I was dressed like that, but that was all. This didn't bother me. After all, I *was* a strange apparition. It didn't hurt to see them nudge each other. Their stares did not feel like a judgement. This discovery encouraged me. I decided to accost someone, a complete stranger, to ask directions, even though I was less than two streets away from home. The gentleman removed his hat and calmly pointed out the route I should take. I then commented on the weather. We struck up a conversation and walked beside each other for a minute or two. When our ways parted, we said goodbye as equals. I was overwhelmed by such joy that just a quarter of an hour later I couldn't remember a word we had said. I felt free and fulfilled. People who have never been judged and written off at first glance must find it hard to understand, but I felt as though I had finally been given a chance to reveal myself. Yes, it was as if my personality became visible only after I hid my face. Or should I say that I only considered myself presentable when I was out of sight?

'Hey, Lady Muck!' a sudden yowl went up. My heart shrank. My newly acquired self-confidence was brittle and shattered at the first blow. Blood rushed through my veins. As usual I took in all the escape routes at a single glance and summed up my adversaries. It was a gang of overgrown louts. Shoulder to shoulder they approached me. One strode out ahead and amused the others by imitating the way I walked. I slowed down and estimated what my chances would be if I made a run for it. They were drunk, that gave me an advantage, but their spirits were high, and fleeing would only encourage them. They definitely wouldn't let their prey escape easily.

'The last head I saw in a net like that was a mackerel!' one shouted wittily.

'Now you mention it,' another agreed, 'it does smell a bit fishy round here.'

While he reaped his success, I realised that their mockery was general. It was targeting the way I was dressed, not me personally. They couldn't see my imperfection. If these lads had encountered someone else in my place, they would have made them their victim. I decided to walk on, wary but determined. For a moment they threatened to block my path and made gestures as if they wanted to catch and gut me, but when I showed no signs of being swayed, their ranks parted and they let me through.

'Hurry up, you're late for the baron's funeral!' one of them called out behind me, and they let fly with a few dirty words, but that was all.

If anyone had told me that public ridicule can be therapeutic, I would not have believed them. But I came home that day a stronger woman. A hymn of victory was running through my mind. The mud that had been slung at me over the years really had soiled me. I had always told myself that the curses and mocking glances were absurd, but this had never robbed them of their ability to harm. Today, for the first time, I had brushed it off. That might seem self-evident to someone who isn't ashamed of his own body, but it came as a revelation to me: others judged my appearance, not my essence. They tried to touch my soul, but came no further than my clothing – garments I had chosen myself. I was the one who had decided to present myself this way and that made all the difference.

I still had to steel myself to venture out again the next morning, but when I did, it was with my head held high. In the weeks that followed I began to build up a small collection. Whenever I heard that a ship had put into port with fine fabrics from the East, I would go straight to the quay to make my selection. Behind the Montelbaan Tower I found a seamstress who sewed veils according to my specifications. Together we designed new models and became increasingly skilful at strategically positioning closely woven pieces to hide my scars while leaving undamaged skin visible and even letting me show my eyes. In a short period, I acquired a number of subtle disguises. They were very eye-catching. *They* were eye-catching, not me. I realised that when you happen to be different, you do best to exhibit your difference clearly. Nothing stands out as much as someone who bends over backwards in an attempt to become something he's not.

My veil had another unexpected effect: on my clientele. Men like to guess. They would rather search than be sure. Any woman can tell you that you stoke a lover's fire hotter by showing him the outline of a hard nipple under taut fabric than you would by immediately baring all. Suggestion is half the work, delay does the rest. With those two skills, a good whore can completely satisfy nine out of ten customers.

The suggestiveness of my veil seemed irresistible. People suspected a mystery and the news spread. I no longer passed a single night without an admirer and their numbers included enough representatives of the better classes. The world seemed to have been turned on its head: instead of waiting to be chosen, I was now able to make my own selection. I chose them clean-bodied and prosperous and not too ugly, and these things made my work much more pleasant, sometimes so much so that I almost forgot that the game was played of necessity. And because *I* was enjoying myself more, my gentlemen enjoyed themselves more. I raised my rates, cautiously at first, afraid of pricing myself out of the market, but more and more exorbitantly once I noticed that the quality of my visitors only rose as I increased my fee.

The more unattainable I made my secret, the higher the circles in which it was discussed. It would be going too far to say that I started a rage, but it is true that around this time so-called Salomes were introduced in several of the better bordellos. These were dancers who satisfied a certain demand by affecting oriental mannerisms and wrapping their faces in thin veils. The error these amateurs all made was to remove their veils when paid to do so, something I never did, no matter how much my clients begged. Each new lover dared to ask at least once, and some of them offered large amounts in exchange for just a glimpse of my face. The more resolute my refusals, the greater and more appealing the mystery.

Soon I reached the stage of being able to confine myself to a number of regulars, gentlemen of quality with whom I felt at ease. Jan Rijgerbos was one, along with Egbert Trip and several other city councillors. Each was allocated a regular evening in the week, which he looked forward to and tried to turn into a special occasion. They knew of each other's existence and each did his best to become my favourite. To assure myself of a regular income and a means of paying my rent, I liked to establish a liaison with a temporary visitor to the city who was prone to loneliness: someone like the Spanish envoy, for instance, or a merchant like Jamieson, wealthy and always grateful.

In this manner, the profession – which I still practised from necessity rather than choice – allowed me to feel valued and cared for. For the first time in years, I was in charge of my own existence. I had everything I needed for a pleasant, indeed a comfortable, life. At the same time, I was not a kept woman, who, even if she is lucky enough to find someone as kind as poor Texeira, remains someone else's property. Now I could refuse if I did not feel like it. I provided for myself and did nothing against my will. And everything I did do only seemed to increase my self-confidence.

It was only now that I went veiled and had taken control

of my own life, that I saw how dependent I had made myself in the past. How I had begged day in, day out, for approval. It was painful to recall how grateful I had been to win the favours of men I would generally have gone out of my way to avoid. And, worse still, the way I had felt when one of those sordid characters had appraised me in a glance and walked on disdainfully to the next in line. After being rejected like that I invariably tried harder, lowering my price and my standards. Only now, with this phase behind me, could I afford to face up to my doubts. Only now did I feel what I had subjected myself to.

I could fool myself that it had been a price I paid to survive. That would be a lie. I recall faces and bodies that made death by starvation seem like redemption. I let them use me. Simply because they wanted me. Physical preservation doesn't explain it. The defeats I see in retrospect seemed like victories at the time. Still busy with one, I would be thinking of the next, like a drunkard longing for another drink. It wasn't lust I was seeking, but affirmation that I was still worth something, that I wasn't inferior to other women. Every time I was done with someone, I felt that my existence had been justified. The hunger I tried to still was more than lack of food. I was searching for a sad consolation, like the one I had first felt in Pasiano, years before, when I let old Antonio, the Count of Montereale, have his way with me.

Now I was able to move on from that. Behind my veil, I rediscovered an image of myself I had thought lost for ever. I didn't see this immediately. For a long time, I was grateful to the world for its willingness to see me differently, whereas the obvious conclusion only recently occurred to me: *I* was the one who had learned to look without prejudice! At last, I had stopped seeing myself through the eyes of strangers. This was the reason for my success, both privately and in love. My happiness no longer depended on what others tossed my way. I now found enough in myself to share it out. The mask

I put on to distance myself actually brought me closer to other people.

Even while undergoing this metamorphosis, I could feel that an important secret was being revealed to me. Within the swirl of new impressions, I caught glimpses of a truth I could not quite grasp, like the feeling we sometimes get at the deathbed of a loved one or on the birth of a child: a sense that this one thing overshadows all else and that, for a single moment, we are looking life straight in the eyes. Obscured by the emotions whirling around inside me like copper atoms in a boiling flask, these fleeting glimpses remained volatile and non-reactive. My new self-confidence was handing me a key to the future. To see it, I needed an antimony, a medium that would cause the precipitation of all the dust that had been stirred up. This clarity would only come to me through Giacomo.

5

'It really is incomprehensible,' he laughs while I nestle down on his chest and relax after our pleasure, 'that some people call this heavenly gift a sin and choose to do without.' He rolls me aside and steps out of bed. I assume that he wants to get dressed and make his departure, but nothing could be further from his mind. On the contrary, as if the job is only half done, he sits down on the edge of the divan, crosses his legs, lays my feet in his lap and starts rubbing them with a gentle pressure that prolongs the last ripples of my lust and makes it surge again.

'People like that really must come from a different planet.'

Giacomo is everything he promised to be. We spent all of that first night in each other's arms. And now, during these last days of the year, he hardly leaves my side. I bask in his attention like a pilgrim luxuriating in a bath, a bed and a blessed conscience after a long journey.

It is true that Giacomo is an exceptional lover: tender and honest at once. He doesn't try to disguise the fact that he is primarily interested in his own pleasure. That is refreshing. He claims, and I believe him, that he can only experience this pleasure to the full when it is completely mutual. That's why he tries to please his lovers as much as himself. This unique approach makes him irresistible. He goes to such lengths that he manages to give me the idea that I have a special place in his heart and am unlike any other woman. This is pure illusion, because at the same time he talks openly of his other conquests. It is strange: full of self-assurance, he discusses the things he gets up to with all kinds of women as if we are at an inn and I am one of his drinking companions. Stories a normal man would deny to avoid ruining his chances, Giacomo deploys to make me like him even more. When our storm has subsided, when we are lying side by side to catch our breath, he shares his most intimate adventures with me. Sometimes he even asks me how I would have managed a particular attempt at seduction in his place or how a woman actually feels when a certain piquancy is proposed in plain terms. The most astonishing thing is that I do not once feel insulted or jealous. He talks to me so openly that I feel as if he sees me as an equal; something I have never experienced with a man before. We are like children, as mischievous as we are innocent, giggling together about the adult matters we discover in our play. 'This is the way things are,' he seems to say. 'These are my pranks. I am telling them to you because I have met my match.'

Equality is an infallible aphrodisiac, but for a lasting effect, both parties must swallow it.

'Fourteen!' he laughs.

It happens on New Year's Eve, our third night together. Giacomo explains a dilemma revolving around a girl he has mentioned several times before. He has recently succeeded in making a great impression on her with his magic squares and pyramids. He finds this Hester enchanting. She is the daughter of Hendrik Hooft, an Amsterdam alderman. Giacomo has been toying with her affections for some time but hasn't dared to take things too far because of her age.

'She will miss your attention now that you are spending all your time with me. And wonder whether you haven't tumbled into one of the canals.'

'I told her that I had to be careful not to see her every day because her eyes were devouring my soul.'

'And she believed you?'

'Not a word.' He shook his head with admiration. 'Only fourteen and already so astute!'

'The fourteenth is a year of great clarity,' I claim as calmly as I can. 'It is one of great impressions and deep tracks. Don't forget that a girl of that age is much further in her development than a boy. At the same time, her innate clairvoyance has not yet been overshadowed by the world. Yes, it's a time when everything she experiences will remain with her for the rest of her life. Please be careful. It is a dangerous age, fourteen.'

Whether he doesn't notice how serious I am or hopes to simply brush my objections aside, he ignores me completely. He relates a daring feat by which he convinced the child of the supernatural attributes of his oracle. She had doubted his cabbalistic skills and had asked him to have his numbers tell her something that no one could know but herself.

'In the middle of the dimple on her chin, Hester has a charming black mole,' he says. 'It is very small, but slightly raised. Like everyone who has been around a little and acquired some knowledge of anatomy and physiology, I know that everything that can be perceived on the face – length, structure, colour and thickness of hair growth, the fullness and shape of the lips – is reflected in the characteristics of other bodily parts that respectable girls generally keep hidden.'

'How wise of you,' I mock, but Giacomo has a firm belief in this old wives' tale and teases me by saying that in my case his source of information is reversed, but he's happy for me to continue wearing my veil, because my body has long since told him what my face is like.

'As I was sure of myself,' he continues seriously, 'I wanted to surprise Hester by making my oracle give an extremely specific answer to her general question: "Oh, chaste beauty, not a soul knows that on the most secret part of your body, that place intended for love alone, you have a little mole exactly like the one on your chin." She was astonished, not because I had guessed correctly, but because she was unaware of any moles on her lower body. So innocent! Soon after, she permitted me to seek it with my hand. When she saw doubt in my eyes, she let me have a look.'

'And?'

'It was there.'

'Of course,' I smirked.

'No larger than a millet seed, but still. She let me kiss it until I was out of breath.'

'And you left it at that?'

'With her, yes.'

His story has excited him. Ready for the second round of the night, he kisses me on the neck and then begins his descent, as if planning to subject me to the same cosmetic investigation.

'What else could I do? Fourteen!'

'That never stopped you before.'

'It did. Fortunately you have left that tender age behind.'

'It's true,' I state, 'nowadays a man has to be something special to make any impression on me at all.'

He takes this as encouragement and I let him have his way, but my heart is not in it. While he loses himself in me, I feel like every move he makes is bumping, shaking and rocking me awake out of the bliss of the last few days.

★

I am not the kind of woman who fails to see men as they are and turns away from them when they fail to live up to her dreams. Without expectation there is no disillusionment. That is the first lesson. It might sound bitter to novices in love, but it consoles the experienced. People are afraid to adjust their ideals. They would rather overextend themselves than accept the toehold they have been offered. That's something I have never understood. You can spend your whole life with your mouth watering, watching a feast you are not allowed to join and stilling your hunger with the crusts the guests toss in your direction. You will die with all your youthful dreams intact, but never once notice the miracle that takes place every day when your empty stomach transforms that cast-off chunk of bread into a delicacy. Anyone can hope for abundance, but what blind faith in your imagination you must have to find hope in deficiency!

This makes it possible for his anecdote about Hester both to disturb me and to do me good. Nothing tempers my dreams better than the cold bath of reality.

'My only worry,' he adds, 'is that the girl will find out that external similarities between the face and the lower body are simply an incontrovertible fact of nature.'

'I don't think that's very likely,' I reassure him. Our bodies are still fused together. I put my hands on his hips and move him to the desired rhythm. 'Because even I have heard it today for the first time.'

'Her faith in me would not only disappear, it would give way to contempt.'

In moments like this I already feel that I am distancing myself from him. Without sorrow, my heart steps back for a better view of Giacomo.

'I'm torn by these anxieties,' he says. 'With you too! The fear that I might lose your respect. Your faith in me.' He stops his play and sits up in bed, genuinely concerned. 'It corrodes the soul to love someone and realise that you are not worthy of them.'

He might be referring to me, perhaps to her. It doesn't really matter.

'So why persist? If you really believe you don't deserve her, why not let her go?'

He looks at me incredulously.

'In view of the gates of paradise?' The thought of not plucking something that is within his reach strikes him as so absurd that his seriousness is dispelled and his playfulness returns. He crawls over the bed on all fours, kneels before me and spreads my legs with gentle fingers.

'Paradise in sight and still renounce it?' Shaking his head, he disappears between my thighs. 'How foolish would you have to be?'

This is the sign I have been waiting for.

I remain Giacomo's lover that whole week, until his departure for Paris on the third day of the new year. Only once is our pleasure interrupted, on the Thursday afternoon when Jamieson appears at my door for our regular appointment. The past few days and nights have merged together so completely that I have lost track of time and am totally unprepared. I make myself as respectable as possible, but it is far from convincing. When I let him in a few minutes later, I still look like something that has been fished up out of the harbour.

'I'm sorry,' I mumble. 'A cold. I'm ill.'

'I can see that,' he says, kissing me and walking through to the living room as always. There, to his surprise he finds Monsieur le Chevalier de Seingalt, dressed up to the nines, sipping from a cup. His performance is more persuasive than my own: he is slumped in a chair like a stuffed dummy, as if he has been there far too long and has had more than enough of visiting this invalid.

'Ah, Mr Jamieson!' He leaps up, seizing his hand. 'At last, some distraction!' Then he hands me the teapot as if it has just cooled off – it's actually been standing unused on the table for days – and asks me to put on a fresh kettle for the guest. This is a man who is accustomed to rescuing himself in compromising situations.

Downstairs in the kitchen, I have time to arrange myself properly and, while Giacomo keeps the American talking, I climb the back staircase and erase all traces in the bedroom.

'But what do you have against the New World?' I hear Jamieson ask as I return with the steaming pot. 'Are you so afraid of the future?'

'Not in Europe. On the contrary. We have turned towards the light and are on the eve of a new era of reason and equality.'

'Aren't the Americas the perfect laboratory to test these new theories of yours, in virgin territory, free of the dark ballast of the past?'

'Our theories have emerged from that very past. We have charted and classified it, and used the results to shape, define and formulate new ideas. This has enabled us finally to succeed in mastering our innate nature. The new growth has just come into bud and is as yet too delicate to be uprooted from its native soil and transplanted. Your continent is in a state of chaos. It has no civilisation and is especially lacking in the tolerance we have won here in Europe through so much struggle.'

'I believe,' I say, while pouring the tea, 'that Monsieur de Seingalt's judgement would be rather less harsh if America had fallen into French hands.'

'That battle is not yet over,' Giacomo says without a trace of irony. 'As things stand, you will have to start from scratch and first reinvent civilisation.'

'Never fear.' Jamieson refuses, for my sake, to rise to the bait. 'A new country with new possibilities and borders that are still expanding. We have at least one advantage over you: we are driven by hope.'

'Yes, that hope of yours, I've heard your compatriots talk about it before. It is a completely irrational optimism, not rooted in the mind like ours, but in the heart. The kind that fuels itself and needs no arguments to become enthused.'

'Just the kind I always rely on,' I interject frivolously to cool the discussion and steer it into calmer waters, where we remain for some thirty minutes. Finally Giacomo suggests no longer straining the convalescent. The gentlemen head off together, each going his own way at the door.

'You have seen so much of the world already,' Jamieson says by way of farewell. 'Perhaps you, of all people, should honour us with a visit, Monsieur de Seingalt. Then you could see the unlimited possibilities with your own eyes. You seem to me the kind of man who would not hesitate to seize hold of anything that might prove expedient.'

'Save yourself the trouble, sir,' Giacomo replies as if he has not understood the insult. Meanwhile he winks at me as a sign that he will reappear on my doorstep after a brief stroll. 'I will never set foot on American soil. Neither the country nor the people bear thinking about. You will never see me there, not as long as I live and breathe, you may rest assured of that.'

To see themselves, people look in a mirror. If they detect something unexpected, they bend towards the glass to inspect the irregularity more closely. I see myself more sharply from a distance.

Whilst being exhibited in the anatomical theatre, I needed to dissociate my thoughts from my naked body and the cadaver that was being dissected before my eyes. The ruin of the body lends the soul wings. Often enough I would rediscover myself on one of the benches in the back row of the lecture theatre. I followed the lesson with the other students. I saw the professor laying bare the corpse's sinews and severing them, before demonstrating the appropriate reflex on the live model – Galathée de Pompignac. I studied the young woman at my leisure and had no need to empathise with what she might be suffering. These were practical and highly instructive lessons.

Later, this detachment proved useful many times in my work when I couldn't stomach a customer or his desire. In the ghastliest of situations, I was able to distance myself. While undressing for one man after another, and letting each watch and touch me, I was sometimes able to observe the whole scene, in which I was the main participant, from afar. It was as if I were sitting in the gods and looking down at the young woman receiving her lessons in love on the stage below.

During my last days in Giacomo's arms, I catch my thoughts wandering in that same direction. I try to drag myself back, but it's so much fun to stand and watch! From a distance, I have a perfect view of my delight and pleasure, and I am grateful that life has given me this chance to enjoy the love I lacked for so long. Then I think of the future and saying goodbye, and the truth, and I realise that observing love is so much safer than experiencing it. I yearn to bring things to a happy end, but I don't know how. One plan after the other rises in my mind while our lustful bodies wrestle, more frantically and avidly as time runs out. Then I suddenly see a chance. I cry out, as lovers do, and gasp for air. Salvation looms up from behind a lectern in the back row of the lecture theatre, high above the bed in which love is being dissected.

For all that I know how to distance myself, I have no talent for goodbyes. My first separation from Giacomo decided the course of my life. Now it's time for a second farewell. Could anything be crueller? And soon there will be another goodbye, at least, if my plan succeeds, if I can find the strength for a third and final parting . . .

Most difficult of all is the night before his departure, our last night together, when we still have time left and can feel it running out. The countdown blocks all pleasure. Our attempt to enjoy every second that remains is so deliberate that we forget to surrender to them. We are perfectly aware of how joyless it is and cling all the more desperately to the next moment, each more fragile than the one that went before. We plunge forward, frantic with desperation, like the boy who drowned last winter trying to cross the frozen IJ too late in the season. If he had stopped, someone might have been able to rescue him, but no matter how much we called out to him, the cracking of the floes under his reckless feet spurred him to run faster, ever faster, ahead.

On the morning of his departure, Giacomo leaves my bed without waking me and hurries off to his lodgings to pack his bags and dispatch them to the post house. I meet him there at ten o'clock, just as his coach is about to leave. If it is unavoidable, then let it be short and sharp. His fellow passengers have already climbed in and urge him to join them.

'And?' he asks with one foot on the step. 'How are you? No regrets? Have I won our wager?'

'Not very convincingly, because I *am* sorry to see you go.'

'From the start, I told you I would not stay long.'

'That is true.'

'And I will be back. Definitely. Maybe even in the spring. You will be here, won't you, waiting for me?'

Those words! I have to steel myself to stand firm. I feel like I recognise every one of them, although I can't be sure they are the same. He gets in. The other passengers' faces! I manage a laugh and raise one finger playfully.

'Shame on you, daring to ask a thing like that.'

'Evidently the answer requires more courage, because you don't dare to give it.'

'I'm not promising anything. I don't want to make the same mistake as your Lucia.'

He is lost for words and can only stare at me.

'Your first love, the one who disappointed you so deeply,' I say by way of explanation. I act as if I haven't let anything slip and try to change the subject. 'You really should know better. I might get a sudden urge to go off travelling somewhere as well. You'd end up holding it against me. No, no promises!'

They close the doors of the coach. He still looks as if he has just seen a ship sailing through the air. I turn to go home. Giacomo is unwilling to leave it at that. He slides down the window and leans out.

'Her name?'

'Pardon?'

'Surely I never said that name? Not in your presence. How do you know Lucia's name?'

The driver lashes his horses. The team jolts forward. The undercarriage creaks. The wheels rattle on the cobbles.

'Easy,' I call out, waving goodbye. 'I know this Lucia of yours!'

6

I have known hunger. Sometimes, when the weather was bad and the fleet was stuck before Texel for a week or two, there weren't enough men for all the women walking the streets of the capital. You could spend days wandering the quays without anyone wanting to use you. I remember this struggle in three phases.

First is the gnawing of your stomach. Concern grows into panic and your body wants everything it sees.

Then lack becomes critical. You have no time for fear or nerves. Like a savage, you scrape around for whatever you can find and shove it into your mouth however inedible. You stop thinking and just take.

Finally nature shows itself merciful. In the face of death, a wave of indifference washes over you. You rise above it all and let yourself be carried along. A blissful peace of mind overcomes you. Instead of worrying about life, you look beyond it. You don't want to have, you don't want to take, you don't even want to hold on. Your beleaguered mind lowers its defences. It opens up. You begin to hallucinate.

This feeling is so addictive that it's hard to be grateful when you are rescued after all. That was why I understood my merchant seaman when he told me about the struggle of men who have been washed overboard. They start off alert, calculating their chances of ever setting foot on solid ground again. Then they become frantic and grab anything that comes near them, often drowning their rescuers. Finally they relax and stretch their limbs in submission, no longer wanting anything but trusting to the water. In this state they are easiest to save.

This is how I was dragged along by love. For a long time I simply believed that to survive I needed to cling to it with all my might.

*

Giacomo was back from Paris in next to no time, even before the thaw had set in. The prospect of a reunion frightened me. I was afraid that it would weaken my resolve, that seeing him again would stir up too many feelings and make me recoil at the last moment from the formidable test that lay ahead. On the other hand, my plan was now so ripe that I longed to put it into practice and deliver the both of us, whatever forces it might release.

Still travelling as the Chevalier de Seingalt, he had moved into the Second Bible inn in the Warmoesstraat and wanted to receive me there in his rooms or, better still, to visit me at home. He was determined to take up where we had left off. In bed. I couldn't do it. His touch would have weakened my resolve. The moment his skin brushed mine, my determination would have flown out the window. A single word, whispered in my ear, would have made it almost impossible for me to persevere. No, I had to make sure that Giacomo and I remained apart until our final confrontation, just as combatants are kept away from each other on the eve of a fight for fear that a single glimpse of the other might summon up feelings of pity and undermine their indomitability. I needed to brace myself with every nerve, with every fibre of my being.

Accordingly, I answered that I was delighted to hear that such a dear friend was in the city but, unfortunately, could not possibly receive him at such short notice. Instead I went out that night with Jamieson as arranged.

The American wanted to celebrate the highly profitable conclusion of his business on the stock exchange and his acquisition of a ten-year monopoly in the Low Countries. He gave me a necklace of black pearls and, despite his rough clumsy fingers, insisted on fastening it himself. The way he struggled to keep my veil down while doing so was touching. We were alone and he had seen all there was to see of my imperfection in the spin-house, so I didn't actually have a secret to keep. He still went to the trouble, just to avoid embarrassing me. I accepted his gift gladly, knowing that it was time for him to take his profits back to New York and resume control of his trading company. He would be sailing as soon as the harbour was ice-free. I would lose my regular income and had no prospect of a replacement. It was almost certain that I would have to surrender my flat, but now, at least, I could pawn Jamieson's pearls to put off impoverishment for a while longer.

I was busy demonstrating my gratitude when an express messenger arrived with another letter from Giacomo. Among other things, he persisted in requesting a meeting because, so he wrote, he had hoped very much that I would solve the riddle I had presented him with on his departure. I put the letter away so that I could return my full attention to Jamieson. He, however, is too perceptive for a man. When he noticed my disquiet and saw that my thoughts were elsewhere, he let me know with a light touch that the show of thanks was not obligatory. Then he stayed just long enough to avoid worrying me further and left so that I could get an early night.

I didn't sleep at all. I took my grandfather's pendant out from where I had packed it away at the bottom of my valise and sat up all night holding it. I refused to be deterred by what I saw. For the first time in many years I looked beyond my reflection and prayed to *Santa Lucia*. I asked for courage, superhuman courage, the kind that enabled her to tear out her own eyes to stay true to her calling and not succumb to the sight of her lover. I brought myself into such a state of ecstasy that, for a few moments, I thought I could feel *her* agony in *my* nerves. Thank God, my common sense returned in time, along with my inborn contempt for women who make meaningless sacrifices. I sat down at my writing table and did what needed to be done, strengthened by the knowledge that I would receive my reward in this life, not the next.

My beloved de Seingalt, chevalier,

Alas. Urgent affairs demand that I depart at short notice for Utrecht, most likely continuing from there after a brief delay to Cologne and possibly further afield. Fate has chosen to hinder the reunion we have been anticipating so keenly. I do not, however, have the right to burden you any longer by postponing the answer to the question that has been on your mind, as you say, since our parting. I presume that it concerns our wager: have you won it or not? As you no doubt recall, it involved two challenges, with the stakes being your reputation and my happiness.

To play the game, I allowed you to win my heart. You acquitted yourself of your task with verve and genuinely convinced me of your love, while remaining open and honest throughout. You never made any promises that you were unable to keep and, upon your departure, the only sorrow I experienced arose from minor expectations I had felt despite myself and despite your lucid representation of the circumstances. As long as it lasted, I was able to give myself over fully to pleasure without losing sight of reality. As a result, I enjoyed our affair and emerged from it unscathed. You can thus count this round as a glorious victory. You have my congratulations, but I can also congratulate myself, because we have both benefited. It is therefore no longer possible for me to pursue my plan of presenting myself as evidence in the second round, namely as an example of someone who has suffered from having loved you.

That is not to say that such a person does not exist.

It was through an unhappy circumstance that she crossed my path some years ago. I met her through several ladies with whom I engaged in small acts of charity for the poor, of whom there are so many in our city. I noticed her face a few times when handing out bread and clothing. In time, she grew less shy. I won her confidence and she told me her story. It was so different from your own — and not only because she called you by the name you were given at your birth — that it took me a long time to realise that my Jacques was her Giacomo and that the unhappy child could only be your Lucia.

She is the ace I have been holding all this time. By playing it, I win, but at the same time I lose, because now that I have grown fond of you, I would rather leave your unswerving faith in yourself intact. I am sorry.

In the event that you and I never see each other again, have no fear. What happened between us was a game that has been played to all satisfaction. You can add me as a credit when making up the balance of your life, confidently crossing off my contentment against the discomforts of she whose existence I could not in all honesty conceal.

Farewell!

Oh yes, if you would like to see her misery with your own eyes, Lucia can be found most Fridays and Saturdays from around eight o'clock in one of the spill-houses on the Zeedijk. Study her first from a distance. I must warn you about her appearance. She is not a pretty sight. Whether you choose to speak to her or not, is a matter for your own emotions, which I have come to trust. In this, listen to the love you once felt. Never pass judgement on a life you have not lived yourself. And be prepared for the worst.

Dare to love,

Your Galathée de Pompignac

I completed this letter towards morning and had it delivered first thing. The rest of the day I tried to rest. It was freezing. For hours I lay in bed listening to the silence of the frost, which lay over the city like an icy blanket, muffling all voices. This kept me calm. Towards evening I put on a patched dress I had bought for this purpose at the rag market. It was tattered and torn; I hadn't worn anything like it for years and it was nothing like my current wardrobe. I didn't adorn myself, except with my grandfather's pendant, which I wore clearly visible around my neck. Finally, at the door, I took off my veil.

I walked to the dike and chose the Gulf of Guinea. It wasn't the worst of the establishments there, but it was still far from salubrious. Not knowing how long I would have to wait, I took a chair close to the fire, where I would catch the full glow of the flames and stand out in the room, which was otherwise quite gloomy.

People were dancing. The regular girls were surprised to see me and had questions, but after a while the novelty wore off and they disappeared upstairs with customers. Only one of them said that my face was scaring people off and ruining it for the rest of them. I responded by grabbing the poker from the hearth, whereupon she fled. The landlady brought me a tankard of beer to calm me down. I sat there and waited, slowly growing drowsy in the heat.

My imperfection. This was the part of my plan I had shrunk from the most: having to show it openly again. Now that I had come this far, it wasn't painful. On the contrary. It had been hidden away for so long that I was struck by the change in my attitude. It would be ridiculous to say that I suddenly derived some kind of pride from my appearance, but at that moment it wasn't a source of shame either. And although I searched for it, the way you might look for a beacon that has been moved unexpectedly, I couldn't find the grief I had always taken for granted. I wondered what had changed about me. I felt stronger, knowing that I would love despite everything. The proof of that was already growing inside me. I just didn't have the words for it yet. And at the same time I couldn't see how this inner metamorphosis could have influenced my attitude to my appearance.

My eyes drifted down to the flames licking at the wood. The flickering encouraged my thoughts to wander even more. And suddenly the drowning man was there again, the one who almost went under by holding tight and couldn't be saved until he let go. Two or three vicious sparks shot up out of the fireplace in that same instant and, together with the branch that was being consumed by the flames, my thoughts blazed. Suddenly, like a saint seeing a vision, I saw the lesson Fate had been trying to teach me.

For too many years, I confused love with desire. Ever since I was a girl, I had seen people yearning. Some went out to hunt for love. Others stayed home, restlessly waiting for someone to come and offer it to them. People talked about it as if it were something you needed. If you didn't have it, you needed to find it. And the sooner the better. If you had already enjoyed it, but lost it again, it was up to you to replace it as quickly as possible, if necessary by stealing the treasure someone else had just secured. Everyone rated acquiring love higher than amassing wealth or fame. Even having a chunk of bread was less important, because love makes you forget hunger. Lovers withstand all deprivations to haul in the prize they have set their hearts on. And no one is as praiseworthy as someone who is willing to lay down his life to win someone else's love.

At the same time, I saw that most people go without. They are pitiable and self-pitying because no one will give them the love they crave. I have known people who longed for a particular person who refused to love them. Meanwhile they rejected the love that was offered to them by people they did not desire. Finally, they grew so miserable that they abandoned their original passion and tried desperately to seize whatever happened to be available. Usually it was too late and they were left empty-handed. Those who didn't set their heart on a specific person were just as unhappy. They waited patiently for the right person to come to give them love. When the moment arrived and their happiness was approaching, they threw the door open and ran out to meet it, arms outstretched at the roadside, ready to finally receive this long-awaited gift. Only to be left completely baffled when the chosen one turned and fled, terrified by so much eagerness. After years in which no one offered the thing they longed for, they fell into a depression, finally losing the only love they had left, the love they felt for themselves.

All of these people, without exception, thought that love was their right and none of them understood why they couldn't obtain it, unless just for a moment.

From the instant I first met Giacomo, I understood what the others were pursuing. I was beside myself with joy. He gave me his love and, for as long as it was permitted to me, it was mine. For years after he left, taking it with him, I cherished its memory, even though I could already feel it slipping away. I carried it around like a little girl walking over the beach with a heap of sand in her hands: as saddened by the amount she loses with every step, as she is proud about how much she has managed to hold on to.

In the end, all I had left were the memories in which I relived the little bit of happiness that had been doled out to me. In my mind I kept running through the scenes in which Giacomo had given me his love. I repeated them to myself word by word. And when I forgot a detail, I made up something else to fill the gap. I put myself in his position and then in mine: in one instant imagining myself as Giacomo, whispering endearments in my ear; and in the next, myself again, whispering into his. Perhaps it was the endless repetition that cast a spell on me, perhaps it was simply studying the same material over and over again that allowed me, like a scientist, to discover an unfamiliar pattern. In any case, suddenly, in the middle of one of my daydreams, I made an astonishing discovery.

It was so simple that at first I mistrusted it. If the truth really was this obvious, why hadn't I seen it before? On the frontispiece of his encyclopaedia, Diderot printed an engraving showing Reason and Emotion together pulling away Truth's veil. She stood before me now as naked and incontrovertible. Was it possible that most people were holding the key to happiness in their own hand and didn't even realise it? Could it be that some things can only be found after you have given up searching for them? Whatever the explanation, I suddenly realised that all of my most heartfelt memories were linked to moments in which *I* gave my love to Giacomo. It was not that I felt less happy or elated or fulfilled when he gave his love to me, far from it, but the overriding emotion then was one of gratitude. Between this giving and receiving of love there was only a shade of difference. During our lovemaking it was negligible and almost imperceptible. I might even have missed it, if fate had not separated us so soon afterwards.

If love is something you get from someone else, you would expect that mine would have ceased to exist once I no longer received it. That didn't happen. It stayed with me. For ever. I experienced my deepest happiness *without* Giacomo, when he was in Venice and I, disfigured, was recovering from my illness. That much was clear. I was never so full of him as in that moment when he was far away from me and I decided to give up my future for him. My love was alive, not because I *was* loved, but because I myself loved!

Now that I understood this, after all these years, I found myself holding the one weapon that can withstand any attack. It is the deeper truth that lies behind the visible, just as the eyes of *Santa Lucia* are engraved on the back of the glass of my pendant and only become visible when the light strikes them in a certain way.

Every word I have written and every word I will write comes down to this. The only reason I am telling you my life is so that you will know this secret from the beginning: we are unhappy because we think that love is something we need from someone else. To be saved we must do something simple that is none the less the most difficult of all: we must give away what we most long for. Not *receive* but *give*. To conjure triumph after all. This is what my imperfection has taught me.

I sat by the fire with a tankard of beer, unmasked, and let my thoughts wander a little longer. If I had been like other girls and rolled from one love to the next without a care, I might have spent my whole life without giving my happiness a second thought. But in that darkness through which I was forced to roam, I was able to catch a glimmer of truth. 'This is my salvation,' I thought, 'and I owe it to this face of mine.'

And slowly I began to feel a recalcitrant pride in my sad burden.

You see a matriarch's wisdom in her wrinkles; a general's courage is visible in his wounds. We are all adorned by the things that have marked us.

'I told you so, Seingalt.'

In the beat of a heart, that cry had me on the alert. It was Rijgerbos. He was standing in the doorway, ready to turn his back on the stinking room after a single glance.

'The only thing we'll find in here is a dose of the clap.'

Giacomo pushed him aside and stepped in.

'You can be mighty stubborn,' Rijgerbos grumbled away in his best French, following his friend as if wading through manure, and taking great care not to touch anyone or anything. 'I don't know who told you to come in here for your entertainment, blast him, but he's no stickler for cleanliness!'

They sat down at the bar and ordered a drink. Meanwhile Giacomo spied out the poorly lit room. Twice his eyes rested on me. I sat there as though paralysed, but it didn't occur to him that I could be the woman he was searching for. Both times he looked away again without any sign of recognition. Finally I stood up myself and approached him. In those few yards, I crossed an abyss that had always seemed unbridge- able. I laid a hand on his shoulder. He looked up in annoyance and gestured for me to leave him alone. It was only after I stood my ground that he looked more closely. My face. My throat. My whole body. My breast with the pendant he knew from long ago. Then my face again, disbelieving. The moment was no less painful for him than it was for me. Tears rushed to his eyes. He turned away to hide his revulsion, but didn't dare to turn his back on me completely. Instead he grabbed his glass to conceal his uneasiness and drained the contents in a single gulp. He sniffed and dabbed his face. Only then did he turn back to face me. I pretended that I was happy to see him again. He forced a smile. I told him that the years had changed him so much I hardly recognised him.

'I am as glad to see you prosperous,' I said in our mother tongue, using the higher, lighter voice of my youth, 'as you must be regretful to see what has become of me.'

'Lucia,' he said finally. 'But I had no idea . . .'

'You *were* told that you could find me here?'

'Of course,' he stuttered, 'I knew that. That's why I'm here. For you. I came because I knew you would be here. But still . . .' Slowly he regained his composure. 'But still . . .' Without taking his eyes off me for a moment, he took me by the shoulders and studied me as if trying to rediscover some of his former affection. Finally all he could come up with was, 'I once loved you!'

To the horror of Rijgerbos, who didn't understand a word of Italian and had stood there gaping at his friend's intimacies, Giacomo suggested that the three of us rent a room upstairs for an hour so that I could sit down and tell them my story.

I stuck to my first lie. Explaining my departure from Pasiano, I dished up the story that I had once ordered my mother to tell Giacomo, inventing a few details to make it plausible. That L'Aigle had seduced me. That I was determined to stay faithful and had tried to fight him off, but that he was simply too strong for me. That I'd wanted to kill myself when I realised he'd made me pregnant, but hadn't been able to bring myself to do it and had fled the scandal instead. That I had fallen prey to loose living and that my body had been ravaged by love. The whole time I was speaking, Giacomo stared at me with glassy eyes. He was so shocked by the way I looked that he couldn't concentrate on what I was saying.

Suddenly, he interrupted me in mid-sentence. 'It's all my fault!' he exclaimed.

I tried to dissuade him. After all, I had gone through this trial hoping to erase both my guilt and his in one stroke. I told him that it could only be put down to Fate and circumstances. Now that he knew that no one was to blame, I suggested, he might be able to understand me, forgive me, at least partly, and then forget me without any regrets. But he hid his face in his hands.

Rijgerbos, still baffled about what was going on, did not dare to look at us. He hid behind a newspaper and rang for more wine.

'If I had come to Pasiano sooner, and I could have – of course, I could have easily – none of this would have happened!'

'If I had really been worth your love,' I argued, 'I would have stayed faithful.' His sense of guilt was galling. I had set up this whole confrontation to stamp out his last feelings for me and extinguish them for ever, not to blow on the embers of his pity. 'I loved you,' I said as coldly as I could, 'but obviously not enough, otherwise I would have put up more of a struggle with L'Aigle.'

'If you had never met me, if I hadn't stirred your passions, your heart would have still been pure when that fellow approached you. You would never have listened to him. If I had been more frivolous with you, or no, more intense, if I had shown you *less* respect, had a lower estimation of you and simply taken you, not only arousing your desires but also satisfying them, then I wouldn't have left you languishing and frustrated, and you wouldn't have needed to give yourself to the first man who came along.'

'Either way,' I said tersely, 'when you came back it had happened.' I didn't want this emotion and tried to keep it at arm's length. But my spirits sank. The sadness in his eyes almost made me cry. Then, just in time, he said something that brought me to my senses.

'God, I was such a fool!' Giacomo lamented. 'For a long time I prided myself on having been so virtuous as to respect your virginity. Now I regret it. I am ashamed of my folly. This strengthens me in my belief that in love you need to take what you can get.'

In a flash, his tone brought our positions back into focus. They had led us so far apart, his path and mine! All I felt was sorrow at the impossibility of ever leading him back to where they had once crossed.

I pretended that I had an appointment and needed to leave. I proposed taking the gentlemen to Giovanna and Danae, so that they could enjoy the rest of the night with them. They did not raise any objections. We said goodbye at the girls' door. I was less surprised by Giacomo's tears than by the growing estrangement I felt, almost as if a great force was pulling us away from each other.

This is where I let go and was saved.

As I was leaving, I heard Rijgerbos snort with relief that the whole ordeal was behind them and they were finally free to vent their desires.

7

The sea is calm. We are into the third week of our voyage. I was just up on deck. I like to see us sailing straight at the setting sun. Everything is painted deep red and the sails look like they're on fire. Then I walk up to the bow and lean out as far as I can over the railing. Poised above the waves like that, I am able to imagine myself completely alone for a moment. With you. I have no regrets. I feel like I have dropped a coin overboard in the middle of the ocean. No matter how badly I might need it, it will sink irretrievably to the bottom, and whatever I do, I will never be able to fish it back up again. That comforts me. What I have lost is beyond my reach for ever. I have no choice but to forget it and sail on. There is no need to be afraid of the future. Nothing about it is certain, except that you are on your way. When dark has fallen, I return to my cabin and continue the story I am writing in the hope that you will one day read it.

No sooner had I left Giacomo after our last meeting – I hadn't even made it out of the alley – before I had to vomit.

This was more than spoilt food, it was violent and deep and came without warning, over and over, all the way home without respite. I spent the rest of that night in bed shivering, as though I were having convulsions. In the morning Jamieson came by. He had arranged his passage and would be departing as soon as the winds were favourable. Realising that he had come to say goodbye, I began to wish him a safe voyage, but he interrupted me, nervously telling me to sit down and hear him out.

'I don't know what's going on with you and that Frenchy,' he started, 'but when he's in town, I might as well forget about you altogether. I do my best, I get spruced up, I bend over backwards to please you, try to be witty, try to look handsome, to catch your eye, but you're off in a world of your own, where I'm as invisible as an Indian in a poppy field.'

'Shame on you!' I laughed. 'If I didn't know better, I might think you were jealous!'

'Jealousy,' grumbled Jamieson, 'another French affliction! Wouldn't exist at all if they didn't cut off their circulation with the elastic in all those ruffles. That's not the point, girl. I wasn't even planning on mentioning it. It's just . . . I like to see you happy.'

I thanked him for the good times we had had together and began to reminisce about one of those evenings, but he wasn't about to be distracted.

'But soon . . . I know what you're like. You're not hard to hurt. What the heck, I've seen it with my own eyes!' For a second, neither of us spoke, remembering the instant he discovered my secret. 'Who's going to be around to stick up for you, damn it? That's what I want to know. And apart from that . . .' He no longer dared to look at me, but began studying his fingers, picking at a nail. '. . . I love women, you know that.'

'And we're all very glad of it.'

'No jokes. I've been around. It's not the first time and . . .

well, to get to the point: it shows. Your breasts are fuller. The nipples are taut. I'm not stupid. It's been a good while since you cancelled any appointments because it was that time of the month. How long have you been expecting?'

'Even if that were so, it couldn't possibly be yours.'

'No,' he snapped, 'I know that. How could it be? I'm a decent man, thank you very much. But everyone knows that the French are a good deal less particular about their personal hygiene.'

'What are you insinuating?'

'I heard that chevalier of yours with my own ears, boasting about, well, you know how men talk when they're alone together, boasting that the new devices that are so popular here only ruin monsieur's pleasure and that he'd rather tie a squeezed-out lemon on the end.'

'It really is none of your business, Mr Jamieson,' I said brusquely, standing up as a sign that our conversation was over. I was genuinely sorry that our friendship had to end this way, but he kept at me all the way to the door, more pig-headed than ever now that he realised he had squandered any chance he might have had by being so coarse.

'I'll tell you once and once only: I know you. I'll take you as you are, past and all, and I – ah, of course, I might just as well say it, what do I care – I don't love you any less because of it, that's what I mean to say. I don't expect love. How could I? Have you seen this mug of mine? Look at these mitts. They're no good for anything. Too big for caresses. Hard from the tanning. I don't have Parisian fingertips that have been manicured all day long. No, I might be able to use them to scrub a hide until it's gleaming and perfectly smooth, but for touching a woman the way she deserves, no, for that they're too rough. I don't have much to offer you, in other words, well, just money, and security, and I could make sure that you and your . . .'

Somewhere in the middle of this tirade I slammed the door on him, but even out on the pavement he kept ranting.

'A lemon, d'you hear me, of all the citrus fruits he chose the lemon and not the orange! Ha! That's the glory of France in a nutshell!' After this he fell silent. I thought he had left, but there was a sudden knock on the door, very respectable and restrained. I didn't open it, whereupon Jamieson, as bashful as if his voice might break, added, 'I just wanted to say . . . soon, when I'm gone, who's going to guarantee me that no one will take advantage of you?'

I can't be sure who your father is. It is as it is. It could be *him*, but it could also be someone else. It doesn't make much difference. I shall love you as I have never loved before, because I have only just discovered that it is possible to do it better. Now I can. I will teach you that as well and, later, when you're old enough, you will read my words and understand why your mother always hammered away at that one thing. Love! It might not seem much, but I learnt it — you know that now — against the odds. In that sense there really is no doubt that you are a child of Lucia and Giacomo. Don't hold too much against them; you are the result of their love.

Jamieson had only just left when a letter arrived from Seingalt. The courier was relieved to find me at home because he had been ordered to deliver it to me at all cost, even if that meant following me to Utrecht, Cologne or even further east. The envelope was bulging. When I opened it, banknotes fell out.

Chère Galathée,

Enclosed please find banknotes to the value of 200 écus as settlement of my debt. You have earned it fairly, although I would gladly have given you ten, no, one hundred times as much if you had spared me last night's disclosure.

Lucia was indeed in the place you mentioned. She approached me. I turned away, but it was too late. She had recognised me and addressed me in dismal tones. Her looks were indescribable. She cannot possibly be more than thirty, but that is irrelevant, she looks fifty or even older, and a woman is always as old as she looks. Her appearance was the result of the gross debauchery to which she had dedicated herself since I last saw her in Pasiano. A courier had impregnated her and taken her to lie in at Trieste, where he lived off her for some five or six months before abandoning her. Anyway, you, of course, are familiar with her sad history. She drained two bottles in the hour it took her to relate it. She spoke most highly of you in the process and I must beg you to continue your kindness to her. She has no one else. I slipped her a few ducats, but if, upon your return to Amsterdam, you can find it in your heart to do more for her, I shall be eternally in your debt. Finally she led us to two girls who work for her, paying her half of everything they earn. As her beauty has disappeared, she has no alternative. It is the classic ending.

Although her downfall occurred beyond my knowledge, I cannot possibly deny my guilt. As a result you win our wager. Poor Lucia, she has not become ugly, but something far worse, repulsive! How heartrending it is to see what we once loved trampled underfoot.

Rest assured of the ardour with which I await your return and our reunion,
  Yours faithfully,
  Seingalt

That same afternoon the wind turned. It didn't take me long to decide. I had already tried my luck north and south. Now it was time to go west. I took a few dresses and packed them away with the jewellery I had left. Because of the unsavoury characters around the harbour, I carried the money from the wager under my clothes. I gathered up what was left of my half-ream of paper, and on those sheets I have now written my life's story for you: the story no mortal has ever heard because I saved it for the one who would be able to love me unconditionally. I was at the quay by half past one, not a moment too soon, because the captain wanted to be out on the sea by nightfall. I used Giacomo's money to pay my passage so that I would not be in debt to Jamieson. When he saw me walking up the gangplank, that big, clumsy man was overcome with joy and cried like a baby. No matter what happens between us, he will be like a father to you. I have his word on that. You will not want for anything.

New York, he says, is now grand and elegant, nothing like Amsterdam. There are some three thousand red-brick mansions. The streets are wide and paved, and lined with sidewalks. The city is so beautiful that nowhere in Europe can compare. It is surrounded by water and broad docks with big warehouses, two of which are owned entirely by Jamieson, one for tobacco and one for skins.

Today we sighted land, probably Virginia. That means one or two days to go at most.

We have made it to the other side.

The coast looks charming, but it seems that life outside the cities is hard. The people in this part of the world are rough but hopeful, and known, so they say, for their unreasonable optimism. As if there is any other kind! According to Jamieson, adversity only makes them even more determined to succeed. I like that: doing things against the current. America has not yet picked up many scars.

Maybe that is what I am looking forward to the most, escaping Europe. That land is too old. It has been wounded too many times. It has been dug too deep. It has been cruelly woken too often ever to drift off into careless dreams again.

Instead it has delivered itself up to reason. Time after time the Europeans have followed their natures and seen chaos result, and now they no longer dare to trust their inclinations. They have grown afraid of the incomprehensible and try, as a result, to lay every last secret bare. Giacomo is like that; he even tries to rationalise his happiness. Forgive him. People can never completely escape the confusion of their age, and I am no exception. For a long time, I too tried to carry the yoke of reason, but it was too heavy for me. I chose to reject it. When you are like me, the last thing you want is to see things as they are. But you will be very different, a product of both, of the old and the new, of heart and mind, and free to choose between them.

I have let go.

I didn't go under.

Postscript

Lucy Jamieson was buried on 11 February 1802 in the churchyard of St Paul's in Flatbush, New York. According to the headstone, she survived her husband by more than thirty years. Three children were born during their marriage. The oldest was a son. She named him Jacob.

Giacomo Casanova never discovered the full truth of Lucia's life and suffering. None the less, he describes her in his memoirs as one of only two women he had wronged. Despite this, he dedicates only a few pages to his first great love. First he recounts their meeting, his feelings and her betrayal in Pasiano. Later he describes the shock of encountering her again in an Amsterdam brothel, where she *had not actually become ugly, but something worse – repulsive.* He seems almost indifferent to how she came to be there or why she gave up her earlier happiness.

Besides the books and archives I used to reconstruct Lucia's story, Casanova's own words were crucial. Like many brilliant people, he has room for different truths in his memory. In his description of his adventures in Holland, where he travelled under the name Seingalt, these truths sometimes clash, just as they do elsewhere in his *Histoire de ma vie*. Names, places, times and even years can differ from the apparent facts. This could be deliberate, to make the story more readable or disguise the truth, but it could also be because of memory's tendency to reorder and reshape events. Giacomo often combines different visits into one, or splits a particular event up over several. From all these truths I have chosen the one that was most consistent with Lucia's story and clarified it the best. In particular I took Casanova's account as the basis for his conversations with Lucia in Pasiano. The dialogue is sometimes identical, but in my version it is always seen from Lucia's perspective. From his memoirs I have also adopted a number of ideas and anecdotes that shed light on Casanova's character and the customs of the day[*]. Other books that proved instructive include Dr D. Hoek's *Casanova in Holland* and J. Rives Childs's *Casanova*.

The life and entourage of Anna Morandi Manzolini have been described by Angela Ghirardi of the University of Bologna. In that same city, Anna's wax self-portrait has been preserved – together with some of her anatomical models – in the Museo di Anatomia Umana Normale. Marcello Venuti himself wrote about the excavations that he and his brothers carried out near Herculaneum. Zélide's flying machines are the life's work of Charles Dellschau. The drawings I describe can be found in the Menil Collection in Houston, Texas, along with the secret recipe for '*soupe*'.

I gained most of my knowledge of the customs and

---

[*] Translator's note: The author cites Theo Kars's Dutch translation. For this English version, I referred to several Casanova translations, in particular the complete translation by Willard Trask (*History of My Life*, Harcourt Brace, 1966) and the selection from Casanova's works translated by Stephen Sartarelli and Sophie Hawkes (*The Story of My Life*, Penguin Classics, 2001).

practice of prostitution in Lucia's day from Lotte van de Pol's magnificent study *The Whores of Amsterdam*, and also derived some terms from a 1681 book with the same title, a detailed account of an excursion to the city's brothels and spill-houses. The classification of whores as horses comes from the mid-eighteenth-century book, *The True Story of Fleeced Farmer Gys*. Once again I was greatly helped by the discussions film director Ineke Smits and I had with prostitutes while researching our film *Whore's Sermon*. I am indebted to these women for the trust they showed by telling us about their motives and experiences, their emotions and their dreams. I am grateful to the Dutch prostitutes' collective The Red Thread for establishing our contact with them. When reconstructing Lucia's sessions in the anatomical theatre and for an impression of the state of anatomy in the eighteenth century, I was greatly aided by Annet Mooij's *Doctors of Amsterdam: Patient Care, Medical Training and Research (1650–2000)*.

Harlequin Hulla, the play Galathée goes to see with Casanova, was written in 1747 by Jacques Japin.